With

Face

Aflame

Aimee Walnofer
Redlands
2018

A.E. Walnofer

Visit the author's website at
http://aewalnofer.weebly.com

Cover design by Julie Hopkins of
https://www.indiebookcoverdesign.com/

ISBN-10: 1717144616
ISBN-13: 978-1717144614

This book is dedicated to

anyone, anywhere

who has ever been moved to ask,

"Why have You wrought me thus?"

You and your story are worthy.

TABLE OF CONTENTS

The Little Wife   1

Above All Else   9

Fetching Eels   25

Nary a Mushroom   43

A Breach of Merriment   61

The Wooing Shoes   71

One Heart Bare, Another Broken   81

Chasing Down the Minstrel   89

'Twas Nice   105

Singing as a Scarecrow   111

Igniting a Flame   119

Straining to Hear   131

Disappointing Thrin   149

The Kiss   159

Gloves in Summer   181

Whelks and Buckets   197

Dancing 'Round the Fire   211

The Queen's Face   229

A Few Coins More   237

A Glimpse of Arches   251

The Minstrel's Sense   265

Wrought Me Thus   269

Asking Such Things   277

For More Ceruse   285

Kicking Rocks   289

An Even Trade   303

Under the Wing   315

After Words   327

An Excerpt of *A Girl Called Foote*   333

With
Face Aflame

The Little Wife

'Twas boots I stared at most often as our lodgers were usually traveling men who wore sturdy footwear. But I also saw the shoes of the upper class, unscuffed and shiny, and the occasional frilled pair of ladies' wear.

That's what I saw before me on this day as I answered the bell's ring. On the left were the feet of a gentleman while, on the right, the dainty tips of a lady's slippers peeped out from under the yardage of a fine, long skirt.

"Welcome to the Gander's Wing of Trivington," I murmured, my face burning.

Why must I be the one to greet them? I wondered as I dipped into a shallow curtsy and allowed the prepared greeting to roll off of my tongue. "For a shilling deposit, I can show you to a fine private room, or a bed in the Commons for a penny per guest."

They said nothing back to me.

I could just hear Babs yammering in my ear as if she'd been there right beside me.

"Lift your head, Madge. Look them in the eye."

But I didn't, of course, as that was back when I didn't do such things. Still, their silence stretched on that I began to wonder if they were from afar off and hadn't understood my words, so up I glanced.

The man, a bit younger than Pappy, was dressed in a fur-edged cape. He had an eerie little smile on his face and his eyes looked hungry. They were staring at my face as hard as I always stared at shoes, and it made me feel as if I was wearing nothing at all.

Though I hated it when anyone gawped at my birthmark – which happened with each new acquaintance – this man's stare was even worse than most. Usually, people looked startled at first and then feigned as if it was the most common thing in England. All the while I had to bluff as if I didn't notice.

Not this fellow. He even stepped forward and tilted his head as if to view my face from every angle, that smirk ever there, as if the color on my left cheek amused him.

I glanced at the woman then, hoping to find safety in the gaze of a member of one of God's gentler creatures. What I saw, startled me. The *woman*, though tall as any adult, had the face of a very pretty child, but it had an unnatural whiteness of the cheeks and forehead which nearly glowed below the wave of her dark hair. Her lips were painted bright pink and on her cheek was a black beauty patch, a small crescent moon, of the sort that fashionable ladies sometimes pasted upon their skin. There were the swellings of a new bosom pushed above the neckline of her embroidered gown, held there by some binding undergarment. She was looking at me, and though I saw sadness in her eyes, there was also a stirring of interest.

Who are these before me? I thought, dropping my eyes to the floor again.

"Hmm," the man said, as though he had decided something about me. "And what is your name, Lovely?"

His voice was low and smooth.

"I'm called Madge," I replied, not used to feeling as if I'd said something naughty whilst answering that query. I wished again that Pappy was there. My face still burned as I cleared my throat and asked, slowly, "Might I show you to a room, sir?"

He flung open his cape, revealing a purple coin purse at his belt, and answered, "Yes. You *might*."

I heard the jangling of coins and then he held one out to me.

Ugh.

My heart sank as I saw it.

"So sorry, sir," I bobbed my head. "But have you a lesser coin? I fear I cannot make change for a crown."

"No need for change," he said quietly, holding it out to nearly under my nose.

Ah. He's one of those who likes to show that money means little to him.

Slowly, I lifted my palm that he might drop the coin onto it, but he did no such thing. He wanted me to take it from his grip, which I did, feeling his eyes still on my face the whole time.

Do you want to sleep here or do you want to just gape at my mark?

The anger I felt made me grab at the coin more roughly than I ought to have. He held onto it for a second longer, then let me have it. After, he said something that made me feel truly ill indeed.

"Make it the finest of your rooms as that is what my wife is worthy of."

His wife*? Is that what he said?*

Somehow, I was able to bob a little curtsy. "Yes, sir. This way, please."

This way to our finest room where you can shut yourself in with this girl who looks younger even than my seventeen years, you smirking sod.

The man grabbed his valise with one hand and his wife's hand with the other and pulled her along. His hard soles, clicking on the wooden floor, sounded as if they were chasing me all the way up to the second story.

Why was I the one to hear the bell?

The clear *ting* of it would hang in the air, beckoning one of us – usually Pappy or Babs – any time a guest rang it. Whenever I heard the bell ring, my stomach would turn for fear that *I* would have to greet the guests waiting in the entry. The actual sound of it was quite pleasant. In fact, Pappy, had chosen a costly bell because he wanted a delicate ringing to be one of the first things guests experienced when they entered the inn.

"The finest attracts the finest, and that's what we want here at the Gander's Wing," he would say. I suspected that his love for finery was why he didn't often require *me* to greet the guests.

The sight of my face might frighten off the finer patrons.

Never did I ask if he feared that, as he would just shush me and Babs would bleat about me pitying myself on account of a birthmark.

On that morning, I had to answer the bell's call as Pappy was away seeing to new signage for the inn's front, and Babs was suffering one of her horrible headaches. When her head was throbbing, nothing short of an invading army would draw her out of her dark, cool room where she sat with a cold bottle of wine pressed against her temple.

And of course, Lottie was of no help with guests anymore as all she did was sit in a corner of the kitchen either dozing or babbling at nothingness.

Ha ha! Maybe I ought *to have sent Old Lottie at the bell's ring to scare away this Smirking Sod. Although, he's such a curious fellow, staring at my mark, that it*

5

may please him to watch the string of spit dangling from her lips.

The thought almost made me smile as we approached the door of the Looking Glass Room. It was our best room, the one with a large mirror that Pappy had bought for cheap after the Great Fire in London many years before.

Lifting the latch, I pushed it open wide, murmuring, "Supper is served at sunset in the dining room."

He had followed me in though the girl remained in the hall.

"The crown will, of course, cover both meals and drinks. Please ring the bell at the desk below stairs if you have need of anything."

Most guests would stand to the side, fiddling with their valise or looking about the room when I said this, but not the Smirking Sod. He was watching me, standing halfway blocking the door. I saw I'd have to brush past him to get out.

"When will the coach toward Spirely come through tomorrow, *Madge*?" He sounded lewd when he said my name and I wished I'd lied about it when asked.

Pappy often drilled me to see if I remembered the various times and pick up points of the coaches passing through Trivington. He said travelers often felt lost and any help we at the Gander's Wing could give eased their minds immeasurably.

"Shortly after sunrise, sir. You can board it just a block up High Street from here at the corner of Water Street."

"Hmm, clever girl," he said, gazing on me a moment longer before pulling the Little Wife in through the doorway.

I'd heard such praise before from guests but said nothing in reply.

Usually, I would have asked if they needed anything before I left, but seeing he was out of the way, I hurried to make my escape. Glancing at the girl one last time as I turned to go, I saw she was leaning against the wall, her head resting on its doorframe.

She looked back at me and her eyes told me, *I've got to stay here with him.*

I'm so very sorry, I thought back at her.

And then the queerest thing happened.

She smiled. Though small and sad, it was a smile nonetheless, and aimed at me. It stayed upon her lovely, sad face as I stepped through the doorway and the man shut the door.

I heard him chuckle from within the room and my feet felt fastened to the hallway floor.

Where is her father? Does he not know of this?

I wanted to fling the door open, throw the golden crown in the Sod's face and tell him to take his vile self to another inn, as we only wanted the finest at the

Gander's Wing. I wanted to grab the girl's hand myself and drag her down to the kitchen where I'd let her sniff all the little spice bottles and pick at the sugared almonds, and we'd talk – about what, I didn't know.

But as I stood there wishing, I knew it was only making me feel ill, so I took a deep breath and went back down to the kitchen, thinking, *I shall make certain she gets a goodly portion of roast tonight.*

'Tis all I can do.

And it sickened me to think it.

.

<u>Above All Else</u>

The next morning as I tidied the Garden Room, the fair strains of a minstrel singing in the market square drifted in through the open window.

What a beauteous voice, I thought, halting in the fluffing of the pillows to listen closely.

The Gander's Wing was on High Street near the town's center, so I often overheard those who were singing for their supper as I cleaned guest rooms. When I knew the songs, I sometimes sang along, quietly of course that I wouldn't be heard by any lodgers. That day was no exception and I joined in, especially pleased at the sound of our allied voices.

When the first song ended, I left the neatened Garden Room and went down the hall, hopeful that I would still hear the minstrel while cleaning the next room.

The Looking Glass Room.

My heart felt heavy as I stood in its doorway, surveying where the Smirking Sod and his Little Wife had spent the previous night together.

That poor girl. Are they truly together today, tomorrow and always, till death parts them?

The room pressed in on me with questions and fears of what had happened there – things I wouldn't want to ask or know even if I could. Outside, the minstrel sang on, but grief kept me from accompanying him.

Walking over to the large four-postered bed, I looked down onto the disheveled blankets. This I did every day to see if they needed to be washed or could just be left upon the bed for the next guest, after I remade it, of course.

That day, seeing their wrinkles and folds made me wonder, as I often did, about what was done under cover of the Gander's many blankets, but this time was different. Seeing a girl nearly my age just the day before and knowing that she had spent the night under *these* covers with a man twice her age doing mysterious things turned me ill.

The thought of *me* being in bed with the Sod invaded my mind. He hadn't been unpleasant in his appearance. In fact, he might have been handsome had his features not been slathered over with such arrogance.

Still, to feel those coin-flaunting hands upon my body...ugh.

Back then, I was still unclear as to what exactly the act of marriage involved. It was just a few years earlier when I had realized that the bodies of women and men were so very different.

It had happened one day when my belly had been aching strangely since morning. I was cleaning myself after having used the pot. As I pulled the cleansing cloth away from my body, I saw it was covered in blood. I screamed, unable to keep myself from doing so.

Babs was there, quick as could be, her hands covered in flour.

I'd dropped my skirt and was clutching my panging gut with both hands, moaning and horrified.

"What?" Babs sputtered. "What's happened?"

Pappy appeared behind her, wheezing like he'd just run out of a burning building. "What's the matter!"

I feel a fool to say it now, but I told them, "I...I'm dying..."

I was remembering how I'd seen our mare birth a colt in the Gander's stable and all the blood that came out of her, so I then said, "I think I'm to have a baby."

That sent Pappy mad.

"Who's done this to you!" He gripped my shoulders and bellowed into my face. "Where is he!"

I started to blub, him crushing my shoulders and hurting my ears. "No one's done anything. Let go, Pappy!"

Babs looked into the pot then and calm as a cloud said, "Hazlett, let go of her. She's started her monthlies, you fool. That's all."

I didn't know what she meant, but Pappy had released me, leaving me bruised and tender. Then his arms were around me and I cried a bit more, but it was a nicer cry.

"You're not gonna die today, Child," Babs said, patting my back.

"Why did you think you were with...with child, Madgie?" Pappy asked, his voice unsteady.

"All this blood and from where it comes." I dragged the back of my hand across my face. "When Fleet was born to Rosie, the stall was filled with it...and then Rosie died."

Later that day, I had two lectures. The first was from Babs and came with a bag of soft cloths. She told me how to staunch the bleeding that would likely happen each month for the rest of my life. She also told a short tale on how babies were formed, though it left me with more questions than answers.

The latter talk was Pappy telling me where to kick a man should one ever touch me unfittingly.

"Aim your foot where his legs come together," he'd said. "There's a foredangler there that God gave men for their own pleasure, and there's a pair of danglers *behind* it God gave for maids to protect themselves from the one up front. Those two bits are the tenderest parts of any man, and if you sink your toes into them, you can stop any man long enough to get out of reach. But the kick must be quick and hard as can be."

Holding a pillow before me, he'd made me practice kicking it, hollering, "Break his hinddanglers, Madgie! Kick! *Aaaand* again!"

He'd kept me at it until I wondered if I'd broken my toe.

"That'll do for today, but I'll drill you on this again so be ready," he'd said.

Now, as I looked down on the mussed bed clothes, I wondered if the Little Wife had ever been taught that lesson and what would happen had she kicked at her husband's danglers when he reached for her. Though there was nothing to be seen on the blanket, I pulled it off the bed into a laundering heap and put it by the door.

Going to the little table and chair under the looking glass, I saw they'd left something behind. It was a small lidded pot labeled 'ceruse'.

Before Old Lottie's mind had leaked out her ears, she'd taught me how to sound out unfamiliar words.

Ker-ooz? Sair-oos?

Not knowing which was right, I lifted the lid and saw inside a clump of white paste.

This must be what the Little Wife spread over her skin to whiten it so.

Looking up from the pot, I gazed into the mirror and looked at my own face. It wasn't something I often did and for good reason – I hated it.

My hair, light brown, hung beside my clear greyish green eyes. My nose was neither too large, nor so small as to look like it belonged to a wee one. My lips were not as full as some I admired on other women, but they were shapely and a shade of true pink.

The features are good but marred by the overlaying of that horrid blighting spot.

Pulling back the lock of hair that I always hung over it, I forced myself to truly look at my birthmark.

Stretching from just under my left eyebrow, it covered my eyelid to the side of my nose, then plunged across my cheek, nearly to my jaw bone. The bottom ended in two rounded parts as if it was paint that had run down my face from my eye. There were varying shades of red in its border and a bit of it had much coarser flesh than the rest.

The first time I'd felt shame about it, I was likely four years of age, standing in the front doorway of the Gander's Wing, watching the crowds go past. It was summer when the streets were full of countless travelers journeying through Trivington. A young man, laughing with his companion as he passed, glanced my way and halted.

"Walt," he'd said, "behold, a little ruby-faced girlie."

Squatting down before me, we'd regarded one another, I as a curious child looks at all things, and he as a man intrigued by a delightful mystery.

A few scraggly hairs sprouted out of his spotty chin. Above a sharp nose, two friendly eyes flitted about. He smelled like apples, one of my favorite things in all the world, and I felt no fear as he reached out with a fingertip to gently trace my birthmark's border. The tickle of it had made me giggle.

"What think you, Walt? If the flesh was incised at a minor depth, would the mark spring back to the surface or be gone?"

"Zooks, Harold!" the one called Walt had said, hardly glancing at me. "Why must your mind always be at thoughts of surgery? Come! I am off to market, with or without you!"

Pappy had come through the doorway then, barking, "Hands off my daughter, you no-good!"

His voice, normally gentle and kind, frightened me, and I began to cry.

"Oh, sir," Harold had shot to a standing position. "I mean no harm. She is a fair child with an unusual mark. I study medicine at university and as of late we…"

"I care not. Leave her bloody stain alone." Pappy pulled me toward him and laid a large hand over the left side of my face. "Now get you gone afore I drub you!"

Peeking between Pappy's meaty fingers, I had seen the two men hurry off without a glance back, my cheek suddenly burning in a strange way. My new, little mind had been startled at the idea that my face was stained with blood. What had seemed like just flesh moments before was actually something Pappy was ashamed of, something he wanted to hide even from friendly people.

"'S'alright, Madgie," he had said, his voice softening back into familiar tones as he took his hand from my face. "Them blighters won't be bothering you again, I venture."

He patted me roughly on the back as I buried my face in his doublet, trying to wipe the mark away on the thick cloth.

I wasn't able to rub it off that day, I thought, looking into the depths of the looking glass. *And here it sullies me still.*

Would this cover it? I looked at the ceruse, recalling the Little Wife's faint smile at me after she was pulled into the room. *Maybe she left it here for such as that?*

A rush of joyful hope washed over me as I imagined myself walking through the market with my head held high, my mark concealed.

No one would flinch at true sight of me!

I dipped a fingertip into the pot and lifted out a blob of paste, leaning toward the looking glass. My hand, unsteady with excitement, reached to trace over the red blotch. As the cool little dab touched my cheek, an eerie shiver overtook me, running down my spine and – although I know I may be thought a veritable loon, I promise this is true – I heard two words spoken as if someone was right beside me.

" 'Tis poison."

Spinning around, I looked in every direction, and saw plainly that I was alone. I stood breathless, my heart thrumming, waiting to see if the curt and sudden voice would speak again.

God?

There came no answer, and I felt even more lonesome than usual for it.

Poison?

Looking back at the blob of paste, I wanted it off of me at once. Grabbing the blanket, I began to scrub it across my face, rubbing my nose raw. My finger, too, I wiped until it burned with cleanliness.

Seeing the faint smear of white on the fabric in my hand, I knew there'd be no carefree walks through the town with the breeze blowing my loose locks playfully across my face as passersby smiled upon me.

Ruinous blemish.

Riveted before the looking glass, glaring at my reflection, I felt a burning, deep and heavy in my chest.

Above all else—above all else*!-- I would be rid of this stamp upon my face that keeps all but Pappy and Babs away.*

A single tear slid down my red cheek and fell from my pale chin onto my bodice.

Nay. Crying is a useless practice. It didn't save the Little Wife from the Sod last night.

Taking a deep breath, I picked up the ceruse and turned to leave the room. But doing so revealed something.

What's this then?

There on the table were stacked three golden coins. They had been hidden perfectly under the little pot.

Lifting the pile, I thought, *They are so very heavy for such small things.*

Flipping one over and holding it up to the light, I recalled the moment my eyes had met the young girl's the day prior.

Right at me she looked, that hopeless smile upon her beautiful face. How kind of her to leave these for me.

My heart toward her warmed from pity to appreciation.

Even in her own distress, she thought of me?

This cheered me a little.

How did she get them? I hoped it had not been through difficulties, shameful or otherwise, as I tied them into the corner of my handkerchief. Tucking the hoard in my bodice next to my thumping heart, I lifted the blanket and the little pot.

Who is *she? Oh! Perhaps her name is written in the guest ledger.*

Shutting the room's door behind me, I hurried down the stairs to the front desk.

Pappy's favorite page of the Gander's guest ledger bore the signature of the Duke of Monmouth. He believed it was authentic, though Babs and I had served the man at table and neither of us was convinced that the fellow who had asked for a third bowl of peas porridge was actually the King's son. Still, that was the page Pappy always had the book open to as it rested upon the desk.

Leafing past it to the page marked June 30, 1681, I ran my finger over the names of guests who had left that morning. In a neat hand, the fourth entry read:

William Porsyne and wife ~ no plans to return

Her husband didn't even think to record her name, poor girl.

Flipping back to leave the book open at Pappy's favorite page, I picked up the blankets and the little pot and headed toward the kitchen.

Babs's arms were elbow-deep in bread dough and Lottie was napping on her pallet, her grey head resting against the wall.

"A pair of slovenly folk this time, eh?" Babs said, eyeing the bundle in my arms. "Too bad. I don't know that Kilta will be here to take any laundry today. Ah, never mind. I need you to go to market."

Ugh! To market?

"You just got back from there! What did you forget that I must now fetch?" The vexation I felt at Babs lightened the lonely confusion I felt still clinging to my heart after my time before the mirror.

"We've need of more eels for a second pie tonight," Babs responded in the sweet voice she always seemed to use when I was frowning at her.

"Babs, you know 'tis a trial for me to go there."

"Each life is full of trials, dear one, yet we all must face them. Oh, and I've a second task for you."

I sighed, exasperated. "What is it?"

Babs tilted her head and smiled. "To sing with that minstrel in the square."

"What?"

Did she hear me singing earlier up in the Garden Room?

I was startled out of my annoyance. But then, the thought of me approaching some stranger—a handsome one at the sound of his voice – and jumping onto the stage beside him to join him in song made me laugh.

"Very good, Babs. I shall run out there and bellow out a tune, if that pleases you."

You wily old crone. blunting the sendoff to market with daft requests.

"Excellent!" Babs declared, staring at me pointedly. "For you have such a lovely voice that the two of you will sound very well together!"

This unexpected praise softened me further and stilled my tongue from arguing more.

She and Pappy are the only two who know I've a fair voice. Well, Lottie made a third, but she knows it no longer.

"At the very least, you must invite him in for a cool drink on this warm day," Babs insisted. "He must be parched."

I thought for a moment before grabbing a basket from the wall and coins from the pantry. "You'll get your eels, Babs, and that is all I shall promise you."

"Madge, he's not a common man. Gaze upon him, then decide if you'll approach him or not, but know that I very much want you to."

Not a 'common man'?

Her words piqued my curiosity slightly, but I simply wanted to be done with the eel-fetching, so I pulled a lock of hair free and strode past her toward the door.

"What's that?" She nodded at the pot in my hand.

"Something a guest left behind."

"Anything worth keeping?" She smiled slyly, probably thinking of the embroidered gloves she'd once found under the bed in the Garden Room, though such finery had no place upon hands that were always plucking chickens or emptying slops.

I wanted to tell her of the voice I'd heard and the eerie feeling the paste had given me but wasn't sure how to say it all. Instead, I held the pot out to her that she might read its label.

"Ooh!" She recoiled. "Get that out of my kitchen!"

"What do you know of it?" I asked, surprised.

"It'll make your hair fall out and turn your gut to rot, that's what!"

Poison.

"Go toss it in the piss pit, Madge. Then scrub your hands with wood ash."

I opened my mouth to tell her I already knew it was dangerous but felt foolish saying '*God told me such*'. My pause got her yelling.

"*Now*, Madge, I mean it!" She was glowering at me as if I'd done something wrong.

"Alright, Babs! You needn't holler!"

Out the door I went and crossed the yard, wondering if I'd feel so vexed at my own mother had she been still living. Babs was good to me, I knew, good to everyone, and Pappy was fortunate in having her as cook for the Gander's Wing, but sometimes she grated heavily upon me.

Most inn-keepers dumped night soils out the windows into the streets to be trampled with all other manner of filth, but not Pappy. He wanted no guest to see the Gander's Wing littered with muck. He'd had a deep pit dug then lidded behind the stables where we dumped the collected waste each morning.

Holding my breath, I lifted the wooden flap and dropped the ceruse into its foul yawn, murmuring a prayer of sorts.

Thank You, God, for sparing my hair and gut.

Fetching Eels

After thoroughly scrubbing and rinsing my hands at the ash bucket in the stable, I left the Gander's grounds and made my way to market.

'Tis a lovely day.

I wouldn't let Babs know that I truly liked to be outside the inn's walls and would be more often if it wasn't for the eyes of all the people walking past me.

'Most of them aren't even looking at you, silly girl! And even if they were, you ought to stand up straight and look right back at them, in the eye.'

Ugh, Babs. Why must you always be talking to me, even when you're nowhere near me?

As I drew closer to the market, I could again hear the minstrel.

'Twould be a joy to sing with him.

I often dreamt of opening my mouth before strangers to raise a song, imagining how surprised they would be when they heard the beauty of it.

Truly, his voice is one of the best I've heard, I thought, though I wished him gone as hearing him reminded me what a coward I was in my very heart.

When I entered the square, I didn't look at the stage where he likely was but headed straight for a certain fish stall. No lodger had ever complained of stomach cramps when the pies were filled with eels bought there, though I thought it was just a matter of time, such vile things they were. I cringed at the thought of flopping them onto the counter to slit down their endless bellies. Yet, it had to be done as guests relished those meaty chunks baked in their pastry coffins. Babs never demanded I gut them, though she often sent me to get them.

"Hullo, Madge," Mark, the stall-keeper, said, reaching for my basket. "'How many t'day?"

I'd bought enough eels from him over time that I'd almost gotten used to looking him in the eye. He was a large man, always propped on a three-legged stool behind his table, with more hair on his arms than on the top of his head.

"Hello, Mark. Three if they're large, four if not."

"Did ya see the Trillin' Runtie?" he asked, lowering three dripping, snake-like creatures into the wicker container.

"I'm sorry?" I asked. "What mean you?"

"That fella there." He waved his wet hand toward the stage. "Not much to look at, but Christ's stripes, how he sings!"

Turning, I beheld the minstrel.

From the distance, I could not see his face very well, but his body was a startling sight. Long legs were topped by a squat torso, as if the upper part of a short man had been stuck onto the lower part of a tall man. His arms, which held the lute he was playing at his belly, were also long, his elbows past his waist. He looked as if a heavy stone had been dropped onto his head, squashing his spine and leaving his limbs unharmed.

"He's the singer?" I asked, though I saw him being so at that very moment.

"Hard ta believe, i'n't it?" Mark marveled. "'S'like milk flowin' from an old hag's tit."

Mark slid the full basket across the counter toward me. Lifting it, I watched the minstrel end his song and give a little bow as he accepted coins from a few onlookers.

Stepping away from the eel stand, I heard the grating sound of Mark clearing his throat.

"Madge, them eels ain't free t'day, nor likely any day." He chuckled. "Stunned by the Trillin' Runtie, she is."

I stifled a sigh, irritated with Mark's thoughtless gibe at the minstrel and with my own absent-mindedness, and reached into my apron pocket for money. "Of course. Sorry."

Dropping it into his large hand, I turned back to watch the minstrel again. Awkwardly swaying side to side, he came down from the stage and walked to a shady place under a tree where a small, grey mule stood hitched to a cart. He patted its side before lowering himself in an ungainly manner to the ground. I couldn't deny that the sight of him resting in the pleasant shade was almost inviting.

He is alone now. But what would I say? Well, I can just get a little closer, if nothing else.

When I was twenty paces nearer, another man strode across the square, headed straight toward the seated minstrel. He moved quickly and in a way that made me wonder at his purpose.

"Ho, there!" He said, far louder than necessary.

I stopped in my place.

"Good day to you, sir," the minstrel replied, standing up.

"Your last song. When I last heard it sung, 'twas in the praise of superstition."

The man was next to the minstrel now, his thumbs hooked onto his belt near where his dagger hung. He then lowered his voice, and I had to get closer, feigning interest in some ribbons at a nearby stall, so that I might hear him.

"What say you to that, Squattie?"

My hand tightened into a fist around my basket's handle. Though Mark had rudely called the singer *the*

Trilling Runtie, it hadn't sounded like a threat as did this.

"Oh no, sir." The minstrel's speaking voice was as clear and pleasant as his singing voice. "That song was my own, written whilst sitting alongside River Cressler last springtime. There's nary a bit of superstition in it."

"Nay, I'm *certain* it sounds much like a song I heard as a child," the man persisted, then continued more slowly. "You ought to alter it."

"Alter it?"

"Aye. Change a few notes." He nodded assuredly, then added, "'Twould please the Lord and safeguard your livelihood." The toe of his boot edged forward and nudged the lute which lay at the minstrel's feet.

I couldn't fathom how the singer responded so cheerfully, "I shall sit down with my lute tonight and consider your suggestion."

"See that you do, as popery is as out of fashion as is your hat." The man laughed as he bumped the brim of the minstrel's hat which fell to the ground. Without awaiting a response, he turned away with a smug smile, and strode off across the square.

"Might I help ya pick the one that best flatters yer colorin' or do ya jes' wanna stand there fingerin' 'em?" The ribbon hawker eyed my eel basket and sniffed the air tellingly.

"No, thank you," I muttered, releasing the smooth length of fabric and turning to fully face the minstrel. He had retrieved his hat from where it had fallen and stood alone again, brushing it off.

A cool drink would do him good.

But I'd have to talk to him.

Then talk to him!

Taking a deep breath, I stepped toward the man.

"Might I offer you a complimentary tankard of ale on this warm afternoon, sir?" I asked, thinking my voice sounded strange, hollow and lost in the open market air.

His mouth broke into a happy grin of clean, even teeth, and I found myself smiling back in spite of how shrinking I felt.

"I was *just* thinking how thirsty I am. I thank you!"

"Follow me to the Gander's Wing, just around this corner," I continued on in the odd voice, feigning a boldness I did not feel.

"I shall. I shall, indeed. Please allow me to fetch Dame." The minstrel headed toward the mule, tottering so that I nearly reached out to steady him. Standing close enough now, I saw that the crown of his head was at the level of my nose.

Once he had slung the lute over his back and held the mule's lead, he stuck his free hand out to me. "I am Keaton of Thorneby, Minstrel to All the World."

I paused, hesitant to touch him, but taking his hand in my own, I was soothed by its warmth.

"I'm called Madge." I bobbed my head, feeling the loose lock of hair flutter aside.

"Is that all?" he asked as we began to walk.

I was taken slightly aback. "What mean you?"

"Surely there is so much more to you than such a short little name as 'Madge'! As we drink, I shall help you form a new title, suitable for future introductions." He said this all with such merriment that it was impossible to feel chastised. "Might I carry your basket for you, Soon-to-be-More-than-Just-Madge?"

"No, thank you." I smiled again.

"Dame's too small to carry a rider, so I shan't hop on her back and gallop off with it, if that concerns you," the man joked, lurching along.

I laughed at the picture of it. "I trust your intentions, sir. But the basket's load is eels and I'd hate to taint your fine doublet with their stench. Besides, my arms are perfectly capable of lifting such a burden."

I cringed inwardly as the last sentence exited my lips.

Please don't think I speak of your ill-formed body! Why must I talk so whilst nervous?

"Dame is the loveliest little mule I've ever seen," I rushed to say, reaching out to stroke her long silky ear that flickered at my touch. I was relieved to see the Gander's Wing come into view. "Ah, here we are."

Wondering what Keaton thought of the inn as we approached it, I snuck a look at his face. He was smiling appreciatively, his head turning right to left to take it all in.

I regarded it myself, the warmth of pride in my chest.

The Gander had a fine front, clean with blue shutters on every window. Fast-growing canes of dog rose were trained up and over the front door, dotted with pink blooms of early summer. The door itself was a lovely sight, built of many narrow wooden planks and rounded at the top.

At that very moment, Pappy was hanging the new sign. He and two workmen were on ladders, setting the heavy thing into place. Pappy had been delighted when he returned the day before with the sign in tow. Made of metal, it would hold up better in all types of weather than the former wooden sign had. Cut out of the metallic sheet was the outline of a large gander, one wing extended as if to draw anyone willing into its scalloped hollow. It was well-rendered and still hangs there today.

"What think you, Madgie?" Pappy asked, looking down from atop the ladder as Keaton and I drew nearer.

"'Tis a revelation to behold, well worth the far travel and cost," I called up to him. "Pappy, this is Minstrel

Keaton of Thorneby. Babs bade me invite him in for a drink."

"Pleasure's mine," Pappy said, descending the rungs and extending his hand. "I'm called Hazlett by all but this fine girl here. So yours is the golden voice I've been hearing all the morning?"

He began to hum a tune resembling one of Keaton's recent songs.

Keaton bowed, seeming pleased. "You honor me with your remembrance, Hazlett."

"Enjoy the ale," Pappy said, then hollered up at the fellow on the other ladder. "Let it dangle a bit lower, Reese!"

"You may tie your mule and cart hither," I said, resting the basket on a tether post. "And we shall go in by this door." I showed him the kitchen entrance which was away from the bustle of Pappy's work.

Once we stepped in, Babs started in at once.

"Ah! She's brought you!" she declared, her eyes and mouth wide. "Here, sit here."

After Keaton had settled himself on a stool, he was soon gripping a tankard full of chilled ale in one hand with the other encircling the neck of his lute.

I picked up a knife and began to dice some onions.

"Ahh...that is the stuff for which I toil," he said after a long draught, wiping his mouth with his sleeve.

"Now, dear lady…" he paused.

"Babs."

"A ha! *You* are the lady who bid me come. For that I thank you." He took another long drink. I saw his eyes drift to the corner where Lottie, asleep again, was propped, her hands hanging lax in her lap. His face remained pleasant.

"Well, if the truth must be known, minstrel, I had hidden reasons." Babs's face took on a mischievous look.

Ah, criminy! What's she got planned?

"Oh, ho! Perhaps I ought to tell you now, dear Babs, that I am soon to be a *married* man!" He lifted his tankard in salute and winked at her.

I bit my lip as Babs's boorish laughter rang out, filling the kitchen as it often did.

He's to be married? *Surely he jests, yet Babs oughtn't* laugh *at such a prospect.*

"Say 'tisn't so!" Babs said, still chuckling.

A sudden snore erupted from Lottie's throat, loud enough to draw all of our eyes her way. She resettled herself, her head hanging forward, her left hand slipping from her lap to rest on the pallet under her. Displays such as these often made me thankful that guests were never in the kitchen. I doubted they would want to eat the fare we prepared there if they saw the daft, drooling woman just feet away in the corner.

Babs waved her hand in Lottie's direction. "Forgive my aged mother. Truly, minstrel, my intention was not unseemly in nature, but rather to coax you into singing a song with my Madge."

"Babs!" I nearly hollered, setting the knife down with a clatter. "Why must you…ugh!"

"You sing, Madge?" Keaton asked.

"Nearly as well as you, she does." Babs nodded.

"Untrue," I replied quietly, though Babs's words sapped me of my anger.

"Oh, ho!" Keaton exclaimed as if he had uncovered a delicious secret, and struck a chord upon his instrument. "Surely you know this one."

He began to sing 'The Maids at Whitsuntide'. Two lines in, he paused to urge, "Join me, Madge."

My mouth opened to protest, my face burning, but as I looked at Keaton, malformed yet smiling, perched unsteadily upon the kitchen stool with the merry tune escaping his lips, I longed to heed his invitation.

Oh, what's the harm? I asked myself and quietly began to sing, though not in the carefree manner common for such a mirth-filled song.

Keaton's head bobbed as we started the second verse, his foot tapping the floor to keep the time. His voice grew and between lines, he called out, "Louder, Madge!"

I heeded him, and Babs began to gambol about the kitchen in the manner of a little girl delighted to be at a country dance.

This nearly made me giggle as I sang to the end of the third verse, thus ending the tune.

"What say you, minstrel?" Babs wheezed, clutching her apron bodice and smiling in triumph.

"Aye, she has a voice to tame any beast in the woods. I drink to you, Madge the Melodious and to you, Babs the Teller of Worthy Secrets!" Setting down the lute, he lifted his tankard and drained it in a few seconds. "Tell me, Madge, with such rich sounds brewing in your belly, why would you not sing always and to all of God's creatures!"

Blushing, I picked up the knife again, and thought for a moment. I knew the answer, but wasn't sure how to speak it. Finally, I shrugged and said, "I don't want anyone to look at me."

"And why not?" Keaton's voice was gentle.

Why not? Surely, he saw my mark. We met under the midday sun!

Slightly vexed, I waved my hand at the left side of my face.

"Because of a bit of color upon your cheek?" he asked. "Many songs celebrate the roses in a lady's complexion. Why, even the Holy Book praises a ruddy beauty: 'As a piece of a pomegranate are thy temples within thy locks.'"

In the silence that followed, I knew he was awaiting my response. Bothered with myself for being irritated with him, I finally said, "My mark is neither a flower, nor a fruit, but a flame upon my face. One that can't be put out."

Babs was silent, wiping the same spot on the table with a cloth again and again.

"Hmm, indeed," Keaton responded. "There are things we cannot change about ourselves."

He sounded so thoughtful at this, that I snuck a look at him. My eyes took in all of him, squat of shoulders, long of limbs, his face pensive, and I suddenly felt ashamed of myself.

"Yet, I've been the world over and you're as fair a maid as any, so smile a bit...and *sing*!" He held his elongated arms out to his sides and began to shake his shoulders comically back and forth, then broke into song.

"I am what I am as I am, sir!
I've nary a wand nor a chant
With which to vary my lot, sir.
I've thought to, but ken that I can't!"

He slid from the stool to stand upon the floor, then capered lurchingly towards Babs, an alluring look in his eyes. Grabbing her hand, he pulled her from the table, the rag flapping in her grasp.

"I'm not the most beauteous fop nor
The richest nor wisest, ma'am
Yet I've got what I've got as myself
For I am as I am what I am!"

Seeing the misshapen man, a stranger only half an hour earlier, dancing around the kitchen with wrinkly, blowsy Babs whilst celebrating himself in song, I thought, *Here is a truly fine fellow. He chides in the gentlest, kindest of ways, making me laugh all the while.*

The celebration was cut short by Lottie. She cried out from her pallet, frenziedly pumping all her limbs like a dog hunting in its dream, looking as if she might fall from her place to the floor. Babs hurried to steady her and spoke in hushed, soothing tones, stroking her arm heavily.

"I am sorry, my lady," Keaton said, bowing toward Lottie's corner, "that my raucous tune has jarred you from your slumber."

He looked so sorrowful that I thought, *I do believe he is serious!*

"'Tis her usual practice, and naught of your doing, sir," Babs replied over her shoulder, still holding onto Lottie's arms.

Though the old woman's eyes remained shut and her body had halted in its jerking and twitching, she called out again. The words, though spoken with a heavy tongue in a lax mouth, were familiar as she had said them many times before.

"Terth-well! Muth get to Terth-well!"

"She thinks she must get herself to Tersewell," Babs explained sheepishly. "There's *healing* there, or so she tells us every now and then."

"Ah, *Tersewell*, you say?" Keaton exclaimed. "I know it. 'Tis less than a day's walk from Thorneby that I call home."

"Truly?" I asked, stunned. "What can you tell us of it?"

"Stories go back centuries, telling of the water's curative properties. How knows your mother of Tersewell, Babs?"

"Her mother spoke of it often as a holy place."

"Ah, the ruinous abbey. Last I passed by there, 'twas overgrown, hardly seen from the road that goes by it. Still, 'tis a lovely place, even in its abandoned state."

The nearby church bell tolled a count of four.

"Four o' the clock!" Keaton declared. "Hmph! If it's up to some, the bells in all steeples would be stilled."

I nearly laughed. "Why would anyone loath bells?"

"Such joyous sounds are an offense to the Almighty, so they say."

Hearing this, I wondered something.

"Is that why the man told you to change your song? He in the square, not an hour ago?" I was embarrassed that my question proved I'd been watching Keaton in the market, but I had to ask.

Keaton replied, "Most likely. In my travels I've met with many who would silence me for what they consider God's glory."

"He was such a nasty fellow. How did you remain so calm?"

"Making one's living in many towns teaches one to be amiable in all places." He smiled. "And I endure it for at summer's end, I want to return home, whole and monied that I might wed my beauteous Jane, the Rose of Thorneby."

Perhaps he is to be married! I marveled.

"But hearing these bells, I shall have to say my goodbyes for now."

"Nay! So soon?" I protested, surprised at my own forthrightness.

"I've a few more coins to earn before getting my supper. I thank you ladies for your kindness, and you,

Madge the Melodious, for joining me in song. 'Twas a great pleasure."

Suddenly, an idea struck me.

"Keaton, we'd be pleased to offer you a bed in the common room tonight in exchange for a few songs in the dining room at suppertime. 'Twould be a pleasure for our other guests. And of course, there's a place in the stable for Dame and your cart."

Though I'd never heard Pappy offer this to another minstrel, I trusted he would not begrudge me this plan.

"Hmm...that is tempting, but I fear I cannot. You see, my traveling companion and I are camping on Wexhall Road, just north of town. He's a bit of a brute – off with a girl as we speak, no doubt – yet I'd not abandon him. But I thank you, truly."

There was the temptation to offer his friend a place as well, but I held back, wondering at Pappy's willingness to host a reputed 'brute'.

With that, the oddly shaped man bowed to each of us in turn, even Lottie who had drifted back into restful sleep, and headed toward the door.

"Will you join us again tomorrow, Keaton?" Babs said.

"Alas! I shall be busking in the towns around Trivington over the next few days, but I shall return here before we head to Wexhall next week, if you will have me."

"Our ale will always flow for you," said Babs.

"Farewell, Keaton," I said, afraid to say more and reveal how truly sad I was at his going. His presence had chased off any of the kitchen's usual drear and I had so many questions for the man!

They shall have to keep until his return.

If he is to return. I'm farewelling the only person I can think to call 'friend'.

You've just met him and can't claim him as such!

But I know we could be friends...

He bowed one last time and stepped outside.

"Well done, Madge," Babs smiled as the door shut, looking pleased with herself. "You sang beautifully. Oh! Did you toss that little pot as I told you?"

It flitted into my mind to tell her what God had said of it.

But I've already got her voice speaking to me all the day. She'd likely claim 'twas her upstairs as well!

"Aye, Babs," was all I said as I picked up the knife to chop again, my throat still buzzing slightly from the song I'd actually sung with another.

It felt a triumph, though a lonely one.

Nary a Mushroom

"Hold still," Babs said, pinning her mother's head back against the wall.

"Nnnnn…" Lottie protested, her arms flapping about weakly.

"Oh, Babs. Leave her be," I said from across the kitchen where I stood slicing turnips.

"No mother of mine is going to have a beard, no matter how short and curly it may be," Babs replied staring at Lottie's chin, then pinching a hair between her fingers. As she yanked it loose, Lottie's yowling filled the kitchen.

"Babs! You pluck them just to make room for more! Besides, no one sees her but *us*."

Still squinting at Lottie's face, Babs said, rather indignantly. "I've been tidying her chin for years. And I'll have you know 'twas at *her request* that I started doing so."

"She wanted you to *then*, but clearly she doesn't *now*!"

Lottie's eyes rolled this way and that, her mouth curled into a confused snarl. All the while, her hands were still pushing at Babs distressedly. It was hard to look at her, old and cronish as she was.

I'll not deny, the hairs abound, nearly enough now for it to be called a 'tuft', but what's to be done?

I heard a sniffle. Babs was turned away from Lottie, her eyes filling with tears.

"Babs?" I asked, startled.

She shook her head and gulped. "I can scarce believe…this is what my mother's become."

All annoyance I felt vanished, and I went to put my arms around her.

"She is much changed," I agreed, sadly.

Babs nodded her head against my shoulder.

But at least you had many years with her, I thought, patting Babs's back as thoughts of my own mother came to my mind. I had only two memories, me being so young when she'd passed.

Mumma's light brown hair fell into her smiling face as she set an egg before me at table.

And then that scruffy, orange cat scratched my hand, and Mumma held me, wiping my nose with the hem of her dress, crooning about '…that big, mean kitty.'

Her name had been Sarah – Pappy always called her 'my Sarah' when speaking of her.

"Ah, never mind, ay?" Babs said, straightening up and wiping her eyes. "Nothing's to be done about it. I've got things to do and an errand for you."

Hoping to cheer her, I was pert in my answer. "I sha'nt be bringing you back any more charming young men, if that's your yen."

"Ha!" The laugh was sharp, but jovial. "Nay. 'Tis mushrooms I need. I'm braising a roast tonight."

"Mushrooms? Why, that's but a pleasure." The heaviness I felt melted away as I thought of venturing out into the woods to gather the budding morsels. There, alone in the trees with birdsong all around, away from the eyes and ears of any, I felt at ease.

"I'll go now."

"See?" Babs said, tugging her apron into place. "Not all my ideas ought vex you. Nor should've the one to invite Keaton here."

I gave her a sideways glance, hesitant to admit aloud that I was very glad I'd heeded that suggestion. But she knew.

Lifting the mushroom basket off its peg, I stepped happily out the door, loosening a lock of hair to drape over my face.

A several minutes' walk through Trivington led me to the town's edge. From there it was the crossing of the stone humpback bridge and past two small fields to the woods. There, the street led away from town but I'd never been beyond this point and wondered often what lay just around its bend.

Ambling into the thicker woods to find the mushrooms for Babs's famed roast beef sauce, I heard a voice on the gentle breeze, hollering out behind me.

"Hare! Come back! Hare!"

I giggled and swung my head around to see a man standing in the field several hundred feet away, cupping his hands around his mouth.

Hunting hares not with a snare but a shout? Methinks his cooking pot will be empty tonight!

The green canopy overhead dappled the light at my feet as I stepped around rocks and broken sticks. Further in I went, delighted with the stillness that now surrounded me, my feet padding along atop the leaf litter on the forest floor.

What did Keaton say? That my voice could tame any beast? That coming from a minstrel who travels afar hearing much singing! He must have liked it very much, indeed!

Looking around one last time at the solitude, I began to sing, softly at first, then slightly louder as the sound pleased me. Away from even Babs and Pappy, my throat could fully relax, allowing songs to flow out as if they knew the way they longed to go.

Finding the spot amongst the Beech trees where there was always an abundance of mushrooms, I quickly filled the basket, singing all the while. The air was cool here and smelled of earth. I filled my lungs with it and sang out more boldly. Several paces away was the stream and I made my way toward it. Slipping off my shoes, I put them alongside the basket on a fallen log and trod across a patch of mud to stand ankle deep in the cool water, my voice bubbling along with the brook.

What must it be like, singing before all the market-goers?

I closed my eyes and imagined myself standing in the spot I'd first seen Keaton, my head up, the flesh across all of my face pale and smooth, some people walking past with appreciative smiles, others stopping to hear me longer, digging into their purses for coins.

I can think of no better way to earn money – no better way to pass time!

'The Maids at Whitsuntide' rang out, bouncing merrily off the trees, much stronger and freer than I'd sung it in the kitchen a day earlier.

Yes, this is how I can sing!

I held some notes and trilled others, delighted at the fleetness of the latter. With eyes closed, I lifted my face to the sun, feeling its warmth on my cheeks and the chill of the water running past my feet.

Suddenly, I was jarred by a splash and something clawing at my shins.

"Oh!" I screamed, then laughed as I looked down to see a little tan dog pawing the front of my skirt. It's longish, black-tipped ears stood straight up and its bright eyes peered at me.

Fear not, 'tis only a dog!

"Oh, my! Whence came you?" I knelt to scratch his head, soaking the hem of my skirt.

But then, something on the bank caught my eye. A male figure in a blue tunic, stood stilly with a satchel hanging on his back.

Gasping, I stumbled back a step, clutching at my bodice, my heart racing.

The man and I studied each other for a moment across the running brook. He was young and lean with a wispy, honey-brown beard upon his chin. His expression was one of wonder, embarrassment and something I couldn't quite describe.

It was he who broke the awkward silence.

"Hare! Come away from her!" His voice was deep. "I'm so sorry he's disturbed you."

With his arm extended and his eyes still riveted on me, he took a few slow steps forward.

"Hare! Ugh, you meddlesome creature!" His feet entered the water.

Seeing this looming figure of a stranger drawing nearer and nearer, broke something in me and I fled. Out of the stream and across the muddy patch, I flew, its pull sucking at my bare feet. Hare ran beside me, yipping and darting about through the splashing and slogging.

"I'm sorry!" he called out. "I didn't mean to halt your song! Hare!"

At the sound of his apology, my terror collapsed into complete embarrassment. Once past the mud, I couldn't keep the pace. The leaf litter, though thick, was not enough to cushion my unshod feet from the pebbles and twigs beneath it and I slowed, then stepped gingerly.

Oh, my shoes! And that was one of Babs's favorite baskets! But I can't go back.

On I continued through the woods at as brisk a pace as my stinging feet would allow, my face aflame with chagrin. Hare was no longer scrabbling along beside me.

That queer look on his face! The memory of the fellow loomed before me, his apologies ringing in my ears.

He meant no harm, didn't follow me into the forest to treat me ill, I thought though my heart still pounded fiercely.

'Twas just poorly timed that I was there in the same place where his dog ran off to. Oh! How must I have looked with my head thrown back, my eyes closed? My face *uncovered!*

My head sank at the thought.

Yet...yet I know the sound of my singing was beautiful. The comfort this brought grew as I pondered the breadth of its truth, walking past the fields and over the stone bridge back to the Gander's Wing.

Yes, 'twas lovely. Why am I so shamed? I want everyone to know how well I sing. Well, now one person does!

But he saw my mark so clearly, certainly.

Treading down the dusty lanes of minor streets and then onto the cobblestoned main streets, which pained my unshod feet even more, I felt nearly hobbled as I reached the Gander's doorstep. Unwilling to yet face Babs and tell her of the lost basket, I went in through the main door, under the newly hung sign.

Pappy was there, at the desk, staring down at the guest ledger with a plume in his hand. He looked up and his face fell. "What's the matter, Madgie?"

"Umm. Well, I've had a fright, but..."

"What's happened?" he asked, dropping the plume and coming around the front of the desk.

"All is well...except I've lost my shoes and a good basket."

"What's this?" Grabbing my elbow, he propelled me to a chair in the little sitting room.

There I sat, the bottoms of my feet throbbing, and recounted to him all that had happened. Though I said nothing of me singing, the retelling was thorough and true.

"Damn Babs's roast sauce!" Pappy said at my tale's end, finally releasing my arm. "You oughtn't be off on your own in the woods! Babs ought to know that! Anything could happen. You recall how to kick a man, yeah? I'll fetch a pillow that you can practice."

He straightened up and turned to go.

"No, Pappy, please!" My great toe had never felt right since he'd first explained to me all of men's danglers. "The man meant no ill. He just..."

"Oh, ho!" he interrupted. "You've no idea what men hatch in their hearts, Daughter. No idea, at all! We're all a bit piggish. I'm ashamed to say it, but there 'tis."

"Well, whether or no, I fled."

"As you were right to do!"

"Yes, but...my shoes and the..."

"*I* will go get them. You go to the kitchen and tell Babs she's never to send you out to the forest alone again!"

His offer was just what I was hoping for though not expecting as it would leave me to greet any guests who wandered in. I quickly described where he would find the abandoned things. I knew the errand would take him a good space of time and watched fondly as he walked out the door, his chest still a bit puffed at my tale.

He's a good man, I thought, thankful as always that Pappy had been spared during the illness which had taken my mother nearly fourteen years earlier.

Could I ever meet a man as good who would want me as a wife?

My mind wandered back to the Smirking Sod and his young bride.

Ugh! Perhaps 'twould be best to remain unwed.

That fellow today, though...such an odd expression upon his face! He looked quite – if I must put a word to it – keen. What thought he of my song?

Thus I sat, lingering on the comfort of the cushioned chair when I was startled by the opening of the front door.

Ah, criminy!

A man stepped inside.

Though my skirt's hem was damp and my feet were bare and filthy, I could not escape being the one to greet him. Sinking deeper into the chair, I watched as he blinked, his eyes adjusting to the dim indoors.

Perhaps if I sit very still, he won't see me. He looks familiar...

With a confident air, unusual for a stranger in a new place, the man looked around and grabbed the bell on the desk then rang it with such force that it nearly hurt my ears. He simply had to look to his right to notice me. To delay my response any longer would be discourteous, yet there was something about him that made me especially uneasy.

That's the fellow who threatened Keaton yesterday! I realized, as I carefully pulled a tress of hair before my face. *What gloom will he spread* here?

Steadying my mind, I cleared my throat and rose from the chair to approach the desk.

"Welcome to the Gander's Wing of Trivington," I said, dipping into a curtsy.

"Where is the proprietor?" the man asked coldly, suspiciously.

I stared at his feet which were shod in boots, though not the rugged type I usually saw.

"My father is away at the moment, but for a shilling deposit, I can show you to a fine private room, or a bed in the Commons for a penny."

"I'm not here for a room, girl. And what's that on your face? A scarlet patch instead of a black one? Such frivolity affronts the Lord."

Stunned, I looked from his feet to his hard, accusing stare. *He thinks my mark a* patch?

"Her appearance is no business of yours, sir," a sharp voice said from down the hall.

Babs was making her ungraceful way toward us from the direction of the kitchen, and I'd rarely been so glad to see her. "Now, if it's lodging you're after…"

"I've already said," the man interrupted, clearly disgusted, "that I've no interest in a room. I must see the proprietor of this property."

"On what matter?" Babs asked, her face set into the mask it held when she was ferociously angry but couldn't let it loose.

"That is none of your concern, woman."

The image of him nudging Keaton's lute with his toe and calling him 'Squattie' shot into my mind and with it a sharp feeling of indignation.

What a horrible man you are!

"As I said before," I said, struggling to maintain courtesy in my voice, "my father is absent presently."

"When do you expect his return?"

"Not for several hours. Possibly not today at all, but we shall inform him of your looking in for him," Babs said, then walked to the front door which she opened wide. "Now if you will excuse us, we have much work to do. The Lord hates idle hands, does He not?"

Bristling, the man looked from Babs to me, then sneered before walking out into the midday sun.

Babs slammed the door shut behind him.

"Damned zealots! Always touting on about how the Lord demands 'good deeds', then treating everyone like shit."

"What was that he said about a scarlet patch?" I asked, my cheeks still burning.

"Don't bury anything that fool said in your bosom," Babs said, pulling the curtain back to peer angrily out the window. "Ugh! He's gone now."

She came away from the window and looked around the entry, huffing. "Where is the basket?"

"Pappy will bring it soon."

"What? Are you returned with nary a mushroom?"

"I've a tale to tell you," I replied, hooking my hand, which still trembled, through the crook of her arm, comforted by the feel of her warm, solid flesh. We headed toward the kitchen.

***

After a short spell, Pappy appeared in the kitchen doorway, a bemused smile on his stubbled face.

"Well, Madgie. I stared at them all the way back but couldn't see the wonder of them."

"What mean you, Pappy?"

"That fellow with the dog, was he wearing blue?"

I nodded, surprised. "He wasn't still there, was he?"

"Aye, on the muddy bank, holding something in his hands, flipping it over, looking at it from every side, measuring it with a knotted string, then scribbling in a little book. I watched him from the woods—surprised his dog didn't bark at me—wondering what in God's name he was looking at, then I realized what it was! I marched right up to him and said, 'I'll be taking my daughter's shoe back now.'"

"What? He was *measuring* my shoe?" I gasped.

"As true as I'm standing here before you both!" Pappy nodded.

"What did he say to you?" Babs asked with a wide grin, lifting her basket from his hand.

"Naught at all." Playfully, Pappy lifted a shoe and squinted at it, turning it over and over in his hand, his mouth lax as Lottie's. "Looking a right simpleton, he just handed it over along with the other one."

He held the pair out to me. I took them, seeing worn spots on the toes and dirty smudges up the sides, wondering what the fellow could have seen in them.

"Why would he stare at them so?"

Was he so charmed by my voice that he thought there was magic in my footwear? The thought thrilled and

56

amused me in a way I'd never before felt and I couldn't help but laugh. Babs joined in with me.

Suddenly, I noticed that Pappy was solemn and silent, his eyes resting on the floor as his hand gripped the side of the table.

This sobered me up quick.

"What is it, Pappy?"

He shook his head and quietly replied, "You sounded like my Sarah laughing just then."

Ah, Mumma's haunting him again. My chest hurt for him.

"That's a good thing, is it not?" I asked softly, walking to him to rest my head upon his shoulder.

"Aye. 'Tis good." He nodded his head thoughtfully, reaching up to stroke my hair. His meaty hand always had trouble being gentle, but I endured the well-meant patting. The moment passed and he turned to Babs, his voice forceful again.

"But *you*, get your mushrooms yourself from here on. I'll not have my girl out in the woods where any dafty might creep up upon her."

"She is unharmed, Hazlett," Babs said. "You want her cooped up here all the time with only you and me to talk to?"

Ugh. They speak of it again!

"She meets and talks to lots of people! Several a day, so says the guest ledger." He stuck his stubbly chin out as he always did when daring someone to gainsay him.

"Asking someone if they want turnips with their roast is not *talking*," Babs retorted dryly.

Pappy turned to me, his voice having lost its certainty. "We're enough for you, aren't we, Madgie?"

My voice faltered as both of them looked at me. I thought of the steady stream of guests we saw daily, always coming from somewhere I'd never been, to get to someplace I'd never go. They didn't seem like true people, but rather people in stories – their *own* stories – that I knew so little about. But here before me were actual beings, Pappy with his worried grey-green eyes, and Babs with schemes ever brewing beneath her frowsy brown hair.

I found my voice.

"Of course, Pappy," I said, but it sounded doubting in my own ears, even as I tried to convince them both – him to comfort him, her to shut her up. "I love you both more than any others."

Pappy looked pleased.

Babs sighed, clearly disappointed. "There *are* no others. Hazlett, she can't forever hide in this kitchen!"

"What's wrong with this kitchen?" Pappy asked, his voice rising. "Nothing but the finest here!"

"I didn't say anything was *wrong* with the kitchen!" Babs shot back.

When they began to quarrel thus, I wanted nothing more than to be away. The row continued as I stepped through the swinging door into the hall, thinking still of my answer to Pappy's query.

Are he and Babs truly enough for me?

I remembered how my tongue had loosened as I talked with Keaton. The ease with which words had flowed out of me made me feel like a different girl. A better, happier girl.

And the fellow in the woods, where was he now? *Who* was he? He who had heard me sing as no other ever had – a truth that horrified and thrilled me in even measure.

Even the Little Wife, with the sad smile aimed at no one but me, flitted into my brain. I had thought of it often and mourned the loss, knowing she mightn't ever return.

All of them were still out there somewhere, thinking, feeling, living, and I felt like a gutted eel, knowing I mightn't ever see any of them again.

A Breach of Merriment

Lottie moaned in the corner, a string of mealy spit hanging from her moving lips.

"Done with your porridge, are you?" I asked, removing the bib from her shoulders, and using it to gently tidy her face. Her hand was frozen into a claw, the nails clipped short, the fingers knobbly and stiff.

'Twas not so long ago that hand was wrapped around mine to steady it in forming letters, I thought, sadly.

Lottie's descent into this state had been swift. Only months earlier – perhaps a year – we would still sit occasionally at the nearby table for a history lesson. When I was a wee one, Lottie had taught me my letters and numbers, then moved on to words and ciphering. By the age of twelve, I was reading Paradise Lost and The Merry Wives of Windsor to her and Babs as they scrubbed turnips or diced suet. Though I preferred the mirthly nature of the latter, she had only the two books, so I handled both quite often. She loved those books, having recovered them from a house struck by plague years before.

"He who bought them couldn't read them again," she'd say. "And their inheritors wouldn't touch them for fear of plague. So I wrapped them in the dead man's cloak and whisked them away though I left them under a tree for a fortnight. I burned the cloak after, but the hardy books are yet here. Now wash and dry your hands well that I may entrust them to you for an hour."

In reading Shakespeare's play, I understood that people in stories were wont to speak differently from anyone I'd encountered at the Gander's Wing. But the beings, both earthly and heavenly, within Milton's poem confused me. There was so much within it I could not grasp though I formed its words perfectly upon my tongue.

"'What there thou seest, fair creature, is thyself...'" I'd read one day, then paused lifting the volume from my lap. "Lottie? Is God really like how He seems in this book?"

"That's Milton's notion of how he is, Child," she'd said, cutting the ends off of green beans. "If you want to know God's true nature, you must read the Scriptures themselves, but I haven't got a volume of those. Now, carry on."

Such a clever woman not so long ago, yet here she was drooling and babbling before me. It grieved me and I often wondered if I'd have learned anything at all had she not barged into the inn all those years earlier. I still remember it though I must have been only six or so at the time.

The Gander's former cook, Edith, had gone to bed one night and never awoken. As I was watching her body be carried out the front door, a pair of women, each carrying a valise, had appeared on the door step.

I had been horrified at the stillness that death required of a body that just the day before had plucked two chickens and baked several loaves of bread.

Pappy had looked worried though those who carried her out had appeared bored, if not slightly annoyed.

Tugging on Pappy's sleeve, I had asked, "Where are they taking Edith?"

"To be buried," he had answered absent-mindedly as one of the men stood before him, demanding payment.

The queer nature of such a statement and the frightening thoughts of dirt being shoveled onto poor Edith's face had made me burst into tears. At this, the two women at the door entered the entryway. One – the younger – had knelt down beside me and put her arms around me, crooning. She was soft and warm.

"Who are you?" Pappy had asked as he counted out two coins into the outstretched palm of the fellow before him.

"I am Charlotte, called Lottie," the older woman had said, stepping forward with difficulty, apparently lame in one leg. "And this is my daughter, Barbara. We know you'll be needing a cook now, which Babs – er, Barbara – does capably, and you've a daughter here who would do well with schooling, which I can provide with excellence."

A look of relief had washed over Pappy's face and he nodded his assent, asking no more questions as if this had always been the plan. Immediately, he had shown the women to the kitchen, the one called Babs holding firmly onto my hand.

From that day on for nearly a decade, Lottie had taught me, rarely smiling, but sometimes voicing her appreciation for my quick grasp on many subjects and mastery of tasks.

Now, I finished wiping thick, sticky porridge off of the gnarled hand of my former tutoress and gently placed it in her lap before taking her bowl to the washing basin.

There was a knock at the outside door.

But Kilta's not due to come for laundry till tomorrow, I thought before opening it wide.

My flood of joy nearly embarrassed me at the sight of Keaton standing on the doorstep. His lute was in the crook of his arm and the bright morning light shone behind him. It had been over a week since his previous visit and I had listened for him through the open windows every day since, not once hearing his fine voice.

"Please do come in," I curtsyed deeply and motioned broadly into the kitchen with my arm, my playfulness surprising me. "To what do I owe the pleasure of your visitation, sir?"

"I thank you, m'lady." Keaton bowed formally, playing along, then stepped inside, a smile on his face.

"Good day, Mother Lottie." He bowed toward the corner from which no response came. "I fear 'tis sorrowful news I bring, Madge, as I've come to bid you adieu. I am off toward Wexhall first thing tomorrow."

"Oh!" I said, my heart falling. "Well, thank you for coming to deliver such sad news instead of leaving us to wonder. I'm sorry Babs isn't here to see you off, but please, sit and I shall pour you a draught."

He settled himself in his ungainly manner upon the stool. "Will you be so generous as to join me in song as you pour it?"

"Perhaps," I said shyly, lifting a tankard from the drying rack with an unsteady hand.

Cease in your quaking! You get to sing with him again! I chided myself, filling the tankard to set on the table beside him.

Keaton strummed a chord on his lute and launched into 'Beneath the Verdant Boughs'.

I resumed washing the dishes, silently at first, but as the song built, my voice rose with his, filling the kitchen. In the last verse, there was a change in Keaton's voice. The notes he sang were different than those that exited my own lips. The introduction unsettled me at first, but I heard how the two parts sung together enriched the song in a deeply satisfying way, and was able to continue on.

"Ah! You *can* hold a melody whilst a harmony's sung!" Keaton exclaimed once the tune came to an end. "Now my heart shall be merry all the morrow, recalling that Madge the Melodious sent me off so well. But here's another!"

He started now on "'Tis Spring in November', which I joined in more readily, still sloshing my arms about in the basin. As the third verse began, there was a knock at the door barely heard over the music.

Kilta?

Drying my hands on my apron, I went to open the door. Upon the step was a young man, a tall stranger, with broad shoulders and a round face.

"Oh," I said stepping back a pace, hating the fluster I felt as my eyes hit the ground. "The inn's entrance is just to your right, sir."

Nearly knocking his head against my own, the man leaned into the kitchen and declared, "Here y'are, Keat! I heard ya singing."

"Brom?" Keaton looked shocked, his fingers stalled over the lute's strings. "Listening at doors, were you?"

Brom chuckled as he stepped inside, standing quite close to me, bringing with him his unwashed body's scent.

"Last week you spoke of free ale at an inn here in Trivington. As I was walking past, I heard your song, then saw Dame at the side there and knew this must be the place. The Gander's Wing, is it?" he asked me.

I stepped back apace from his looming frame. "Aye. That is where you stand, sir, in its *kitchen*."

"Brom," Keaton spoke. "Never did I state that free ale flowed here for any who knock upon the door."

"Nay, but surely for friends..." Brom ducked his head toward me as I ventured to glance at him again. I caught a flinch in his eyes as they flitted over the left side of my face.

"Will you not introduce me to the lady, Keat?" he asked, studying me in the uncomfortable manner with which I was familiar.

"Madge," Keaton began, the edge of irritation in his voice unabating, "this is Brom the Juggler, my traveling companion. Brom, this is Madge, with whom you are *not* to meddle."

"Of course!" Brom chuckled again. "Pleased to meet you."

"And I you." I nodded.

And when will you be leaving, sir?

A silence followed and I noticed Brom's attention was turned to the tankard on the table beside Keaton.

"Do you fancy a draught of ale?" I asked, knowing the answer and wondering what Pappy would think of me giving away drink to strangers who barged their way into the kitchen.

"Aye," Brom nodded, then settled himself unbidden upon the stool next to Keaton as I poured it.

He appeared unaffected by the uncomfortable quiet as he lifted the vessel to his mouth. After a long swig, he smacked his lips appreciatively.

I returned to my spot at the basin and was put only slightly at ease when Keaton began to softly strum his lute. He did not sing and the joyful mood of the kitchen only moments before had vanished. Though comforting, Keaton's strumming had a mournful quality.

Soon, Brom was roughly setting his empty tankard upon the table, looking around the kitchen with a pleased, shameless expression upon his face.

Daren't you ask for a second draught, sir, I thought, wondering at the bounds of this fellow's impropriety, but Brom said nothing, his eyes settling on Lottie in her corner. He stared dully at her for a moment before Keaton ended his song and spoke.

"We have trespassed upon your hospitality long enough, dear Madge," he said as he stood. "Brom, I trust you, too, have things to tend to before we leave tomorrow."

Brom grunted in agreement and rose from the stool.

"I thank you for the ale, Madge, but more so for the song and the amity," Keaton said as the two men made their way to the door. "Should you desire to sing anywhere in England, I would be fain to do so by your side."

My heart felt heavy at his words.

Keaton might have stayed longer had this rogue not come knocking.

"You are welcome any time your travels bring you near," I said quietly, taking the hand that Keaton held out to me.

"I trust that goes for both of us," Brom laughed while he stepped outside.

"Hm, you're a very *trusting* fellow," I said under my breath.

Keaton snickered, pausing in the doorway. His eyes locked with mine.

"I'm sorry," he mouthed silently.

I shrugged and smiled a little.

With that, both men were out the door, gone from my sight and ready to pursue whatever adventure awaited them. I secured the latch and returned to the wash basin – the same place I stood washing a hundred or more dishes every day – wondering why Keaton, the finest of men, would bother befriending, let alone traveling with a dolt such as Brom.

The Wooing Shoes

Later that afternoon, I was upstairs sweeping a room when I heard the sound of raised voices in the entryway below. Leaning the broom against the wall, I crept down the hallway toward the staircase to listen.

"Under whose authority?" Pappy's voice boomed.

"The Lord's, of course!" another voice declared, not as loudly. "Need you ask such questions?"

It must be that horrid man – he who thought my mark a patch.

"God does *not* begrudge weary travelers a bit of ale."

Though I couldn't see him, I knew Pappy was standing, his face purpling as the largest vein in his temple throbbed. I crept closer to look down on the scene and prove myself right.

The zealot's back was toward me and it seemed that he was not as upright and proud as the last time I'd seen him. He continued solemnly, "And another woe – last time I came here, two women greeted me. 'Tis unseemly for all it suggests. A time is coming when such lewdness…"

"A time is coming when I'll wallop you," Pappy interrupted. Then his voice dropped low. "And that time is nigh."

I knew he was sincere. The man seemed to understand that, as well, and after a brief moment left without another word.

Once the entry door clicked shut, I went downstairs to stand at the desk. Pappy looked at me silently, and shook his head in disgust, his face slowly resuming its usual color. Though I knew what could have happened had the man not left, I couldn't help but smile at Pappy.

"What did he want?"

"He said I'm to serve no drink but small beer at table." He rested his hands, balled up into fists, on the desk. "He fancies himself the Lord's orator."

I'd never told Pappy of the ceruse or how God's voice had warned me of it. It was such a different message than that of the departed zealot.

"Why would he deem himself worthy of being such?" I asked.

"He's not the first fool to deceive himself in that."

"Perhaps wine is acceptable? Did you tell him you'll meet with a wine merchant tomorrow in London?" I joked.

"Ha!" Pappy laughed and beckoned with his hand. "Call him back. I'll let him know!"

Suddenly, there was the creak of the entryway door opening again. For years I'd fled at that sound and did so now into the adjoining sitting room. I was fully behind its wall as footsteps crossed the wooden floor to the desk.

"Welcome to the Gander's Wing of Trivington," Pappy said, a remnant of ire still in his voice. "How might I help…ah, I recollect *you*."

The last words fell flat as if the remembrance was a disappointment. I longed to peek around the corner to see who was nettling him now.

"Good…good day, sir," a deep, though timid sounding voice began. "I am called Yates of Lethwood and I've come to…that is, I would like to…"

"Yeah?"

There was a yip and the sound of scratching just outside the entry door.

Yates took a deep breath and started again. "Last week, I unwittingly frightened a young woman whom I believe lives here."

The fellow in the woods? He who heard me sing…

"I've come to make amends for causing her alarm."

"No need," Pappy responded, curtly. "She is perfectly sound. But tell me this, Yates of Lethwood, how came you to know where to find her?"

With my heart pounding in my ears, I pressed my face up against the wall and leaned out just enough to peek at this Yates fellow. He was dressed in that same blue tunic and stood before the desk with a sack in his hands, his shoulders slumped forward.

"Oh, well, after you came for her shoes, I, umm, I watched where…"

"You followed me." Pappy interrupted.

"Uh, aye. I did. Please, sir. Might I explain? I'm apprentice to Hodges the Cordwainer—he can vouch for me – well, last week he'd sent me off to Wexhall, and that's when I came across your daughter." He began to open the sack. "I felt ill at the fright I caused her and have brought her..."

Oh, let him continue! I caught Pappy's eye over Yates's head and looked at him pleadingly.

He stuck his tongue out at me as Yates pulled something out of the bag and placed it on the desk.

"I've crafted these as penance."

He's made me shoes?

Though I could not see them clearly, I saw Pappy's face soften into something close to appreciation. He reached to lift one from the desktop and flipped it over, examining it closely.

"These are a fine pair," he said. "But 'twould be unseemly for a girl to accept such a gift. What would it imply?"

"N-nothing, sir, I assure you," Yates continued. "And they're crafted exactly for her foot from the measurements I took."

Pappy bit his cheek and shook his head.

Don't send them away! My hands itched to hold them as I leaned further out from the wall.

There was another yip at the door, followed by a mournful yowl.

"Hare! Quiet!" Yates snapped, whipping his head toward the door, and in my direction.

I had grown careless in my spying and our eyes met as I darted back around the corner, but not before I saw his face change from frustration to surprise.

Damn!

For the next horrible moment, all I heard was my heart pounding in my ears and the stupid sound of Pappy quietly chuckling. My face burned as I curled up against the wall as small as I could, waiting miserably for either of them to say something.

Pappy's gentle laughter stretched on unbearably and when Yates spoke, his nervousness had lessened. There was even a faint note of amusement as he said, "Please sir, even if she's not to wear them, allow me to leave them. They're of no use to me."

"They don't fit *you*?" Pappy joked. "Fair enough, Yates. You needn't return them to their sack."

"Thank you. And…please, sir, might I…might I…"

"Might you what?"

"Uh, might I…ask your daughter's name, if you please?"

"Margaret."

"Well, please wish Margaret well from me."

"Aye, that I will do," Pappy responded.

Hare yowled a third time.

"Ugh, vexatious dog," Yates muttered. "Good day to you, sir."

"And you."

I heard the door open and shut.

"You can come out now," Pappy announced.

I emerged from the anteroom, glowering as he began to laugh out loud.

"Oh, hold your joggling belly. 'Tisn't funny! Now he knows me not only as a woods-runner but an eavesdropping-peeper as well! And why did you give my name as 'Margaret'? I hardly recognize it as myself."

"You *are* 'Margaret', as God and everyone present at your christening knows. Now stop bickering at me and come look at what he's brought you."

Still embarrassed, but eager, I went to the desk and took the shoes in my hands. Holding them up to the window's light, I saw they were very unusual indeed, nearly flat and floppy, but finely wrought.

Even stitches of thick thread secured the smooth brown leather into a foot shape. This upper portion was sturdily attached to a thick, leather sole with more tidy stitches. Running my hand under the bottom, I felt it was fashioned out of rough, knobby skin whereas the rest was smooth and supple. Two toggle ties fastened it together at the ankle. I loosened them to peer inside at a soft insole.

It was not the delicate footwear of a lady, nor the cloddish shodding of a farmgirl. Rather, it had a rugged elegance, beautiful in its simplicity and careful design.

Pappy began to chuckle again.

"He woos with shoes, the dafty," he said.

"Oh, Pappy, still your tongue," I replied though I couldn't keep a small smile from my face. "He's just fretful over the fright he caused. No need to claim he's come acourting."

Still, 'tis much ado when a simple 'sorry' would suffice.

I bit my lip, picking up the other shoe to examine it just as closely.

"You had better try them on," Pappy said.

"But you said 'twould be unseemly!"

"I had to make him sweat a bit."

"Such cruelty, Inn Keeper!" I said, laughing. Heading for the nearest chair, I kicked off my slippers and fastened the first, then the second, of the new shoes onto my feet. I stood and walked across the entryway, feeling a slight give in the leather around my heels with each step.

"With thicker hose they'd fit without flaw," I announced, turning on my heel to saunter haughtily across the space again as I'd seen a few of our wealthier female guests do.

"So they're a winter pair then," Pappy said. "Or a traveling pair. You planning a journey, Madgie?"

"Hmm, aye." I leaned against the desk and bit my knuckle. "In these shoes, I shall march all the way to London." I laughed.

"Would you like to go there with me tomorrow? See a bit of the world? Babs could bring in Kilta and her sister to help run the inn for a couple of days while we're gone."

"Hmm…" I shrugged, not wanting to decline outright, though I didn't much fancy the notion.

"Well, think about it. Anywise, Yates'll be pleased to see those on you when he returns." There was a sly look in his eyes.

My heart began to beat faster. "What makes you think he'll return? He's apologized and delivered the shoes."

"What do you think he was stuttering about at the end there?" Pappy looked at me, knowingly. "He wanted to ask if he could come back to see you, but couldn't get it out, so he settled on just asking for your name."

"Pappy, don't say such things," I murmured.

Could it be true?

"I can spot a restless buck when I see one. I don't like it much, but I see Babs is right that you ought to know more people. I know Hodges and he wouldn't apprentice a wolf, so this Yates fellow may visit you here where I can keep my eye on him. But don't go meeting him out in the woods!" He shook his finger at me.

The teasing tone in his voice had changed, sounding forced and uncomfortable.

"I wouldn't. You know that."

I felt his eyes on my face, studying me before he suddenly flipped open the guest book on the desk as if to read a page in earnest.

The sudden change in his mood struck me as odd, but I was so delighted with what was upon my feet and the notion that their maker may soon return that I hurried off to the kitchen to tell Babs all of it.

.

One Heart Bare, Another Broken

"What's the bother, Hazlett?" Babs asked Pappy as I dried what I thought was the final dish of the evening.

"No bother," he replied, standing at the pantry with a list in his hand, taking inventory of all that filled it.

If Yates does *return, what ought I to say to him?*

As I placed the bowl in the cupboard, I imagined his face before me and my mouth opening to spill out words, hopefully not too stupid.

'Thank you for the lovely shoes. Oh! And sorry that I spied upon you.'

Feeling foolish, I shook my head, then glanced to see if either Pappy or Babs had noticed. I didn't want either of them to ask what I was thinking about. Neither was looking my way as I hung the damp towel on its peg near Lottie's corner, taking more time than usual to arrange it.

I could ask him about his dog. If 'twasn't for that dog, I'd not be wearing these at present.

For the hundredth time that night, I looked down at the shoes upon my feet.

"Are you sure, Hazlett?" Babs asked.

'Why'd you name him Hare? How long have you had him?'

"All is well, Babs," Pappy responded a little sharply.

Ugh. Is an argument brewing between these two?

Turning to face them both, I announced, "I'm off to bed."

"Have you decided if you'll go with me on the morrow?" Pappy asked.

I wrinkled my nose at him, still unsure.

What if Yates returns tomorrow and I'm not here to greet him?

"You needn't decide now." Pappy said. "I'll knock on your door at dawn. If you'd like, come along. Otherwise, I'll see you when I return."

Kissing him on his bristly cheek, I bade Babs good night and patted Lottie's clawed hand, then went through the swinging door to the hall. It swished silently shut behind me.

It had been a very busy day with the visits from Keaton, the zealot and Yates, as well as many guests wanting rooms and meals. I was exhausted.

Traveling season has begun anew.

As it was the start of summer, the steady stream of people would only increase over the next few months until the harvest required most to work in the fields.

My heart was still light from the day's earlier events.

Why would Yates bother himself to craft such things for me? I wondered, wiggling my toes within the new shoes as I walked.

Perhaps the beauty of my song overrode my face's lack of it?

As I passed the dining area, there in the dim firelight I saw the tankard and trencher of a lone, tardy lodger left on a table.

Ugh. I thought I was done! I lifted the dishes, glanced around the room for any others and padded back down the hallway toward the kitchen.

Weary, my push on the kitchen's swinging door was slow. The sound of hushed voices on the other side was so unfamiliar and fervent that I halted in place.

"But Madge is a hard-working and wise girl," Babs said.

"I know this and needn't be reminded," Pappy answered, his voice not harsh in the chiding.

"Well, what mean you then?" Babs urged.

There was silence for a moment.

Lingering in the doorway, I held my breath.

What troubles Pappy?

"I...I've found that..." his speech was thick and slow. "It has grown difficult for me to...to look upon her face, such as it is."

The doorjamb seemed to tilt and the floor pitched beneath me. I clutched the dishes to my chest as I tipped toward the hallway and slid silently down its wall to the floor. The swinging door had fallen back into place, damping the voices beyond.

He can't...he can't look upon my face?

There was a roaring in my ears. I raked a hand across my left cheek, my fingertips rubbing over the coarser skin of the mark.

Damn stain!

Then, as suddenly as I had lost my footing, I was up and rushing away as quietly as I could. Flying up the stairs to the second floor, I then ran to my room. Flinging open the door, I dropped everything in my arms and fell onto the bed, sobbing.

Pappy doesn't love me anymore?

Nay! 'Tisn't what he said.

My mind was flooded with proof of his care, his concern, his tenderness.

'Tis only my face *he loathes.*

The memory of Lottie's twisting, hairy face as Babs plucked her chin rushed into my mind and fresh sobs racked my body.

Am I to end like her, drooling in the corner – no one wanting to see me? Why must I live so lonely – friendless in this stupid inn – and now, even my father thinks me disgusting?

Damn, damn mark!

I writhed upon the bed, my head aching with grief, recalling how Pappy's eyes had fallen from my face to the guest ledger earlier that day. *I cannot stay where I cannot be looked upon.*

Oh, to be rid of this hateful spot! But how?

A memory stirred in my mind, and with it, a new notion.

Lottie spoke of that holy well.

But she's daft as a loon!

Not always. She was the wisest of women not so long ago. Before she lost her mind, I remember she spoke of Tersewell. As did Keaton. And he knows where 'tis! He said he's leaving on the morrow for Wexhall. If I was to go with him, likely he could lead me to Tersewell, then I could be home within a few days.

But leave home? Leave Pappy? And Babs? What of Yates?

Yates be damned! I pain Pappy each time he sees this wicked spot. That will never change if I stay here!

"God?" I whispered, my eyes burning with shed and new tears. "Ought I to go?"

You warned me of poison. Will You not speak to me now? That my father cannot even look upon me feels deadlier than a little pot of white paste.

Silence.

I've money from the Little Wife. That would keep me fed. And shoes for a journey delivered just today. Are these things from You?

Though I strained to detect any stirring of a whisper, I heard only the clatter of my own thoughts. I lay thus all the night, thinking, pleading, planning and crying more than ever I did in my life. Just as the light of dawn began its banishment of night's darkness in the square of my window, I heard footsteps in the hallway.

"Madgie?" Pappy whispered from without. He didn't try to open my door. At his urging, I always fastened it tight that no errant guest could enter my chamber. I lay very still as he once again, a little louder, called my name. After a pause, he walked away and down the stairs, the floor creaking in his wake. There was the faint opening and shutting of the front door, before I rose from my bed. Peering out the window, I soon saw him ride out of the stable, his hat pulled low over his ears, saddlebags bulging on Fleet's hips.

Goodbye, Pappy.

He'll be gone for two days, at the least, thinking I'm here with Babs. And Babs will think I've gone off with him to London.

I watched him until he was out of sight, my heart exceedingly heavy, then dropped a few things into a sack, including the money-filled handkerchief and a waterskin. Shod and dressed, I bundled up a couple of blankets and crept down the stairs to the entryway. By now the light of the rising sun was brighter coming in through the window by the front desk. Pausing there, I opened the ledger to a clean, new page at the back and hastily scribbled upon it.

I am safe and will return when I am able. ~ Madge

Babs won't see this as she never bothers with the ledger. When will Pappy find it?

Doubting two days was long enough to get to Tersewell and back, but hoping four would be, I shouldered my belongings and exited the Gander's Wing, leaving it and all within it, behind.

Chasing Down the Minstrel

The sun was well overhead and my throat was dry with thirst as I rounded another of the countless bends of Wexhall Road.

Arriving at the campsite common for travelers just as the sun broke over the eastern hills, I'd spotted Keaton and Brom as they readied themselves for their trek. Keeping my distance, I followed them from there. Brom's height and Dame's sluggish pace made it easy.

Once I am past that bridge, I will make myself known to them, I decided, gazing off into the distance. *That will be far enough from Trivington to show that I truly want to join them.*

Wagons, coaches and those on horseback passed me, going in both directions, stirring up dust in their wake. I didn't know how many curious glances I received from the many other travelers on foot as I kept my eyes to the ground, only looking up now and again to see Keaton and Brom. Today I pulled my hood low, concealing not only my birthmark, but also my eyes and nose swollen from a night of crying.

Soon, we had passed the bridge but I continued to trail behind, deciding to hail them once we'd passed a dead oak which stood beside the road. That site, too, came and went, and I did not quicken my steps to meet them.

Keaton bid me come.

That was nothing more than the friendly farewelling of people parting. He might scowl at the sight of you here and now. You could be back home before dark.

Nay! I couldn't bear to face Pappy. Onward.

But what will you tell them? How ought you explain you've left home to follow near strangers to places unknown?

In the little time I'd spent with Keaton, I felt I could tell him, at least in part, the reason for my journey, but how to say it, I knew not.

Ugh, I'm so parched! I clutched my waterskin, now limp and empty.

In the early afternoon, it was my growing thirst that finally drove me to make myself known to Keaton and Brom. They had left the road and settled onto a fallen log, pulling victuals from their packs to munch upon.

With legs so shaky I marveled that they moved me forward, I slowly approached the two men.

Brom saw me first.

"Damn me, Keat!" he laughed. "A wench has chased you down! Might you owe her a shilling?"

As Keaton turned, the severe shock on his face was not what I had hoped to see.

"Madge! What brings you…is all well? How came you…?"

All my planned words melted away as I saw him, dumbfounded, stuttering in wonder at my appearance.

Dreading how stupid it sounded, I simply said, "You said you would be fain to sing across the whole of England with me by your side."

Pathetic! You sound as if you're accusing him or begging him! Neither is fair.

"Uh…I'm off toward Spirely and beyond," he said.

Brom interrupted, guffawing loudly. "Never shun a maid who's followed after you, Keaton, unless she's squawking about you having gotten her with child."

"Brom, shut your stupid mouth!" Keaton shook his head in disgust, then turned back to me. "Madge, won't Babs worry? And your father…if he thinks I've convinced you to this, he'll hunt me down and hang my head from that beloved sign of his!"

Oh! You didn't think what risk this might be for him!

Brom laughed again.

"Keaton, I said nothing of you in the note I left, and…and 'twill only be for a couple of days."

"But I won't return to Trivington till next summer."

"You needn't accompany me back. I know the coach routes from various towns."

He pulled his hat off and twisted it in his hands. "Madge, when I said you sang well, I meant it, but I never thought 'twould tempt you to this."

Shoving the last bit of his meal in his mouth, Brom stood and moved off to the nearby woods with his back to us, appearing to relieve himself into the brush.

My heart hurt that Keaton thought he was at fault in some way.

I must tell him something more.

"I won't go back, Keaton," I whispered, shaking my head. "I cannot. Tell me not to follow you and I will leave you now, but I won't return to Trivington. Not yet."

My voice broke on the last bit.

The minstrel's eyes opened wide. "Madge, what has happened that you…?"

"I shall explain later," I said. "But for now, please tell me if I must leave you or no."

Keaton shook his head. "I couldn't turn you away. I just don't understand…"

Brom lumbered back toward us, fastening the front of his breeches.

"...never mind for now," Keaton said. "Come with us into Carfmore. Have you had any dinner?"

He held the torn end of a loaf of bread out to me.

I declined, my stomach too knotted for anything solid. "But might I have some water?"

"Of course." He handed me his waterskin and I lifted it to my lips. As the cool wetness began to pour down my throat, I was unable to lower it until it seemed half of it was gone.

Brom scoffed, laughing. "Keat is small, but he still needs some drink for himself, Kitchen Wench."

"Sorry," I murmured, ashamed at how light the skin felt in my hand.

You're draining him already, and this journey has just begun.

"No matter," the minstrel replied. "Thirst is a power none can tame."

As is grief, I thought, handing the skin back to him.

***

"Have you been to Carfmore before, Madge?" Keaton asked as we entered the town's square a short while later.

Surrounded again by throngs of people as we walked along, I felt my shoulders hunching forward. I shook my head.

"Well, 'twas a good place to sing for supper last year but let not the success we have here fool you into thinking all places will prove as bountiful."

A stone dropped into my stomach.

Sing for supper?

Of course, simpleton! You told him you'd come to do exactly that!

Within moments, Dame was tethered to a post and Brom was juggling multiple colored balls drawing in a crowd. Sitting on the ground, I looked up at the glints of color as they flew rhythmically up, then down into his hands, perfectly. Pretending I was there only to watch him, I tried not to notice the crowd grow as more people gathered.

Keaton sat nearby, plucking the strings of his lute and adjusting its knobs as the sounds pleased or displeased him. After a moment, he finished and said quietly to me, "You see, we attract crowds for one another, Brom and I. He may be a lout, but he's a helpful one. Join me in the second verse but stand that you can sing when it's time. Ah! Here is my cue. Now watch this..."

With a mischievous smile, Keaton was on his feet and approaching Brom from behind. He swung his lute as if it were a common club toward the juggler's backside.

The people in the crowd laughed as Brom yowled and all of the balls fell to the ground around him. He clutched his buttocks with both hands.

"Scoundrel!" Brom hollered, shaking his fist at Keaton who now posed with his lute, looking unworried as he drew his fingers across its strings.

At the first chord of 'The Maids at Whitsuntide', Brom seemed to fall into a trance, and Keaton began to sing. To and fro Brom swayed with a dullard's grin upon his face as Keaton circled him, playing and singing. Soon, Brom's feet started to move in time to the lively tune until he was dancing wildly as if under the music's spell.

Brom's ability to play to the crowd astonished me.

Who'd expect this from such a clod?

I watched, amused along with all those in the crowd, until Keaton turned toward me and nodded his head.

The second verse!

My throat seized up as I heard the song circle around. At the end of the first line I ought to have sung, I had made no noise and Keaton glanced at me questioningly though his own voice and fingers did not miss a note. I nodded back at him, my heart in my throat, and opened my mouth again to sing.

The words wouldn't come. I stood there before the crowd, my cheeks burning, knowing I looked a fool as my jaw and lips worked in time to the music, birthing no sound. A couple more glances from Keaton, and I knew I had completely missed the second verse. Soon, he was well into the third and final verse and had ceased to look at me altogether.

He finished the song with a merry "Hey, ho!" and Brom was released from his dancing spell.

Glaring at the minstrel menacingly, Brom dropped to one knee and picked up a red ball. Cocking his arm back as if to throw it, Keaton struck another chord and Brom froze.

The song he now began had a melancholy tone and soon, the juggler was feigning weeping, clutching the ball to his chest and looking up to the heavens, swaying all the while to the mournful tune.

The crowd continued to laugh at this change in Brom as I sank to the ground next to the cart, my failure bringing tears to my eyes.

How can I expect to travel as a minstrel if I can't sing?

At that song's end, Brom, himself again, pulled off his cap and walked with it outstretched and belly up, around the edge of the group that had gathered. Several people dropped a coin or two into its depths.

"Mumma! Mumma, look at the funny little man!" a small girl pointed at Keaton, laughing.

I flinched, dismayed that the mother did not hush her child, but rather laughed along with her.

A broad smile flashed across the minstrel's face and he bowed with a flourish to the little girl and her mother as if they were royalty. "At your service, m'ladies!"

"God bless you, sir," the mother replied, tossing a coin to him, and laughed more as Keaton began to dance an ungainly jig.

Within moments, the crowd had shrunk and Brom sat on the ground near me counting out the coins he'd collected. As the last onlooker moved on, Keaton, winded from his dance, leaned the lute against the cart and plopped down beside me.

I couldn't meet his eyes.

"I'm sorry…" I began.

"Were you afeared, Madge the Melodious?" he asked gently.

I shook my head and lied. "I couldn't remember the words."

Keaton's voice was full of doubt, but kind. "Hear me now, Madge, you've a lovely voice and perhaps you fancy the thought of singing to make your living, but 'tisn't an easy way. We minstrels sleep rough, many days eat light, and suffer crass treatment aplenty. Brom mayn't like the delay it causes, but tomorrow I shall accompany you back to Trivington."

My heart leapt in my chest.

"No," I protested. "I won't be going home. Not yet. I *will* sing. I must."

Keaton dropped his voice. "What're you not telling me, Madge?"

Peering pointedly toward Brom who was stacking the money into two even stacks, I shook my head.

"Keat," Brom said. "What say we both throw in for a chicken and some abricotts for tonight? Here's yours."

He began to toss coins to the minstrel, one at a time. His voice took on a teasing tone. "I'd likely be throwing a couple *your* way, wench, had you done aught to earn them."

Keaton bristled. "Don't chide, Brom. She was…"

"No," I cut in. "He's right. I did nothing and deserve nothing."

There, that shall urge me on to do better tomorrow as I don't want to humble myself before the likes of Brom every night.

***

That evening, we settled into a stand of trees just outside of Carfmore. The sun had set, but there was still enough light to see well around the site. Brom and I were sitting near a fire he had built, he licking his fingers of the juices from a roasted chicken. In my hand, I held a chicken leg, long cold, that Keaton had insisted I take. The one bite I'd had of it had turned to sand in my mouth.

I've done nothing but take all the day.

"Are ya gonna eat that or jes' stare at it all night?" Brom asked.

Wordlessly, I handed it over to him.

Keaton was picking through the cart, pulling various things out of it.

With his mouth full, Brom stood, declaring, "I've a cart to unload."

With that, he wandered out into the woods chewing on the bare chicken bone.

Though I was confused by his words, I was nonetheless relieved to be left alone with Keaton at last, even if just for a moment. Getting up, I went to stand beside him.

"Keaton," I said softly, "I've money to pay for my supper." I reached into my bodice to retrieve the handkerchief of coins.

"Keep it, Madge." He shook his head, then beckoned me. "But come sit by the fire. You must tell me why you are here."

I looked over my shoulder in the direction Brom had gone.

"Don't worry. He'll be awhile. His bowels are always stubborn at being emptied."

We sat down in silence that lasted for a long moment.

I can't tell him I seek healing at Tersewell. He'll think me terribly stupid.

Yet, I can't go home.

"What's happened, Madge?" Keaton's hand rested on my shoulder. The weight and warmth of it heartened me slightly. "Surely 'tis not your love of singing that has driven you from home."

True as I couldn't sing!

A sense of panic descended upon me and my eyes began to well.

Damn these tears! And Brom could return at any moment. I must tell him now.

My words came out as a fierce, jagged whisper, "My father…he said that he couldn't…"

I paused, just trying to breathe.

"What did he say, Madge?" Keaton asked, gently.

"…he said he could no longer…look upon my..."

My throat tightened, the word stuck there. With my hand quivering, I motioned toward my mark.

"Nay!" Keaton exclaimed, throwing his long arm around my shoulders and pulling me towards himself. "He couldn't have!"

Tears streamed down my face as I nodded.

"That man who hummed my song and shook my hand, said such a thing? Is he oft so cruel?"

Realizing I had confused Keaton about who Pappy was, I rushed to explain.

"Oh, nay! He is loving…the dearest father I could imagine. He'd never try to hurt me. 'Twasn't to *me* he said it but to Babs, in the kitchen when they thought I'd gone to bed."

"Hmm." Keaton's arm loosened a bit. "I do understand. My father is also a kind man, but…"

He paused, staring into the fire.

"When I told him that Jane and I intended to wed, he looked at me as if I'd lost my mind and asked, 'How can you be a *husband*?' There was no malice in the words, but they were barbed in my ears. I didn't let him see how they wounded me.

"I knew not what part of husbanding he doubted me in. Did he mean I couldn't get food for the table? I couldn't carry my wife out of a burning house? Couldn't sire a child? I walked away from him with my head held high and determined to prove him otherwise, though I cried for hours alone afterward."

Within the comforting crook of his arm, I listened intently as Keaton continued.

"I spoke with Jane – she had already agreed to marry me – I told her the only way I could see 'twould be possible was if I traveled during the summer months to try to earn the same money a farmer gets at harvest. She agreed to wait for me."

Sweet Jane!

"Well, last year I started out for the first time and arrived home with about half the money of what I'd aimed for, but 'twas enough to give me hope that if I did things differently this year – stayed longer in some towns, and away from others altogether – it all might go apace for me. Father agreed that if I returned in late September this year with a certain amount that Jane and I could marry and live in the cot on the family farm, make a home of it. Thus I save every penny I can and stay amongst crowds of people that I'm less likely to be robbed.

"So Madge, I *do* understand how a father can love you, but break your heart with a word. *And* I fathom your determination to prove yourself."

Prove myself?

There was a rustling of leaves and Brom stepped up to the fire. "Keaton, ought ya to be touching a girl? Yer Jane'd be angry, I venture."

Though I didn't look at him, I could hear the grating tease of his voice.

Oh, you horrible Brom. Why must you return at this moment?

Hearing Keaton's story had brought fresh tears to my eyes, tears of sadness for his grief. Tears of relief that here was another person – a good man – who had felt the deeply stinging words of poorly aimed truth. It made me trust him even more, though the last bit of his speech troubled me.

Yes, Keaton, I see you must prove you can earn money to keep a family, but what could I do to ease Pappy's pain at seeing my mark?

With Brom looming nearby, I could say none of this.

"Oh, I see," Brom started again as he drew closer, looking at me. His tone changed from teasing to knowing. "The Kitchen Wench is weeping as that's how girls are."

"Yes," I said simply, wiping a hand over my wet face. "That *is* how we girls are. And now, this girl would like to go to sleep. I wish you both good night."

The two men murmured responses. Keaton squeezed my shoulder before dropping his arm to his side and I stood. I arranged my blankets into a bed a few feet from the fire. Removing my shoes, I laid down and hugged them to my chest, pulling the top blanket over me, hoping Brom wouldn't notice and question why I held them there.

He wouldn't understand why these shoes mean so much to me.

Staring up into the night sky, knowing I was vulnerable to endless and sundry harm sleeping out in the open, I marveled that I felt neither afraid nor uncomfortable.

Though the ground is hard, heart pain blunts all other feeling of mind and body.

Can I be a minstrel? Today makes me doubt it sorely. And healing waters? Can I believe in such things?

Yet, I can't return home knowing that Pappy loathes the sight of me.

God, I know I heard You in the Looking Glass Room that day. Will You not speak to me now?

I lay as still as I could, the rise and fall of my chest my only movement, straining to hear anything beyond the sounds of an English countryside slipping into nighttime. Waiting that way, exhausted and sorrowful, it was suddenly morning, and I felt none the wiser.

'Twas Nice

"You've said you don't like the eyes of a crowd upon you, Madge," Keaton said as he sat on the fallen log, polishing off an abricott left over from the night before. "And since your mind is set on traveling with us, I've an idea to free your voice. But none of that will matter if you know not the songs. Today is not a travel day as I found it good to perform in Carfmore *two* days last summer. Therefore, we have time this morning that I might teach you what you ought to know. Come, sit beside me."

Brom snored on the ground nearby, his blanket kicked off almost completely.

We'll wake him if we sing.

As we ought. If you can't sing before an uncouth lout, whom can you sing in front of?

I don't know that I can do this.

You must, or go home to hide your face evermore.

Wiping sleep out of my eyes, hoping to hide the heaviness of my heart, I sat down beside my cheerful friend.

"Keaton, last night you told me how you came to be traveling – thank you for telling me your story, by the by – but how came you to sing at very first?"

A thoughtful look came over his face.

"My grandfather was often called upon to make music at weddings by those in Thorneby and beyond – this was his lute." He patted the instrument affectionately. "'Twas discovered that I sang well at a young age and he would take me along. I soon found that I felt the happiest when I sang, when many eyes were upon me, all lit with a glow that only beauty can ignite."

He can bear to be stared at, even with his odd little body?

I couldn't understand it, but then, the memory of Yates in the woods flitted into my mind. My heart warmed at the recollection of the look upon his face.

He looked wondrously pleased, though embarrassed at having caught me.

"I grew keen to live in that moment as oft as possible," Keaton continued. "There were minstrels who would at times busk in Thorneby, and what joy was mine when I was told again and again that my voice put theirs to shame! So when Jane was foolish enough to fall in love with me, it seemed the obvious answer for me was to set out with my lute. My father lent me Dame. You see, he is a kind man."

"Were you not afraid to go?"

"Ah," his face lit up. "If you knew my Jane, you'd understand that I'd skip forward to face dragons to gain her hand. And now, Madge the Melodious, you have kept us long enough from our task. You must learn these songs."

I breathed in deeply. *I must sing. Whether it sounds good or bad.*

He lifted his lute and began to play. "Let us warm your throat with one you know."

As Keaton started to sing, I joined him immediately, though quietly.

"Louder, Madge," Keaton encouraged with no hesitation of his fingers upon the lute's strings. "I need to hear you clearly. And fill your belly with breath that you will have much support there for each note."

I obliged, staring into the ash of the fire pit. Into the second verse, I felt my throat relaxing, easing the song's escape.

He's right about the deep breaths, I thought, noting how much stronger they made my voice feel. *And we* do *sound nice together.*

Keaton dropped into the harmony.

By the third verse, I was almost enjoying myself.

Why can I not feel this at the first note?

When the song concluded, Keaton exclaimed, "Well done! Exceedingly well!"

A shadow fell across my face and I looked up to see Brom standing, his lengthy frame stretched and tense in a silent yawn, his hair wild. Blinking in the new sunlight, he muttered thickly, "'Tis true. 'Twas nice."

Taken aback by his kind words, I wondered what to say in response. But before I could speak, he lifted his leg and loudly broke wind.

"Ah." He clutched his stomach and stumbled off toward the woods muttering, "I've another cart to unload."

Keaton chuckled as I was frozen in disgust, staring after the juggler. "Well, you've heard it directly from a grand gallant such as he. *'Twas nice.* Come, let's try another."

For another hour, we practiced, our voices rising together into the morning air. Occasionally, travelers upon the road went past, but I would not more than glance at them. Three songs in, a woman leading a small gaggle of geese stopped a moment. As I saw the outline of her form from the corner of my eye, my throat froze.

Sing through it.

And so I did, forcing the sounds up and out of the pit of my being, cringing as I knew they faltered. Suddenly, the many geese began to honk, raising a din that filled the forest around us.

"Quiet, you lot!" the woman barked uselessly at her flock.

Oddly, I found the racket heartening and Keaton and I smiled at each other as we sang on together, me with more certainty.

At the song's end, the woman's voice rang out again, happy this time. "A lovely morning anthem! Thank you!"

A kind word in spite of the rough patch.

"Good day to you, lady and to every one of your geese!" Keaton responded.

Daring to turn and look, I saw her standing amongst the tall white birds as they milled about, a swishing stick in her hand. Her cheeks were pink in the cool air, and a smile lit her face.

I waved, my chest warm with feeling pleased and answered, "Thank you!"

"Carry on then," she called, brightly, and started on her way, swinging the stick to herd the geese onward.

"You see, Madge?" Keaton asked, wiggling his eyebrows comically.

"Hold your tongue, sir," I said softly, smiling down at my knees.

Perhaps I can do this.

I thought back to the moment before I'd fled the woods, leaving my shoes behind. I'd sung so freely and beautifully. *Yates wouldn't have bothered to make shoes for a girl who sounded like a yowling kitten!*

Or would he? Perhaps he's just a very good soul who shows kindness to those he pities most?

Nay! I do sing very well!

Looking at his hand, Keaton stood and declared, "My fingers are done for the morning. And now we shall go about piecing together your costume."

"My *costume*?" The joy I felt fled.

"You've said you are shy to be *seen*." His face took on a mischievous look again. "Perhaps a disguise while busking will embolden you."

Won't something as gaudy as a costume glue every eye upon me?

If this is his plan, you are bound by duty to at least try it. You've no better ideas to offer.

This disheartening reasoning held my tongue.

"Come," he said, walking to the cart to rifle through it. "Between Brom's things and my own, you shall be dressed."

Singing as a Scarecrow

Keaton's plan is failing.

I am failing.

And this shirt smells of Brom's sweat.

Some of the straw Keaton had stuffed in the hat's crown was slipping past the collar and the itching was driving me mad.

I peered past the floppy brim of the hat, my heart thrumming in my ears. We were back at Carfmore's market. A few people had gathered at the stage's edge and by the sounds all around me, I knew there would soon be many more.

Are they looking at me?

I couldn't tell as the brim dipped down to block most of my sight. My mark was well covered, I knew, and all I needed to do was remain still through the first song, but my legs felt weak as water.

Breathe. Slow and steady. In and out.

"Brom will be dressed as a farmer," Keaton had explained, his eyes glowing, "and he'll carry you across the stage to lean you against a pole. You must freeze in place that the people will think you merely a stage prop.

Then, once Brom starts his angry-farmer bit, you will join with me in singing, quietly at first that all may wonder whence the sound comes."

"Yes, that may work," I had murmured, picking through the clothes he'd pulled from the baskets in the cart.

"See here?" Merrily, Keaton had lifted a pair of Brom's rough-cloth breeches, a mischievous look on his face. "These are exactly the sort of cast-offs a scarecrow would wear."

Now they hung from my frame.

Keaton's doing all of this for kindness to me, I thought as he walked across the stage and into my sight. Black feathers plucked from supper the night before were stuck into his hat and doublet. *Even willing to put on his own silly guise, though he looks more a chicken than a crow.*

He is too good to me. If I can't sing today with this ridiculous garb on, I ought to just walk back to Trivington in it.

Keaton strummed the first chord.

Cued thus to begin his act, Brom stooped in front of me and adjusted my hat as a finicking farmer setting up a scarecrow might.

How is he so at ease? I marveled, thankful for the supportive pole behind me.

Ugh, Brom. Your breath! I tried not to flinch as his face hovered inches from my nose.

The marketplace filled with song, and the crowd grew. I watched warily from under the hat, knowing that soon, something more would be required of me than to simply stand pretending to be a scarecrow.

And now, they spar.

Farmer Brom began to chase Crow Keaton around the stage, waving a stick and hollering in feigned anger, drawing out laughter from the crowd.

How can such an uncouth brute as Brom alter himself thus, sometimes to be admirable and others loathsome?

Then there was a break in their skirmish and Keaton started the second song.

My stomach lurched anew as the chorus approached. I took a deep breath and a few sung words squeaked out at the right pitch but sounding as if a cord was tied tightly around my throat. Still, I sang on.

Eventually, I relaxed a bit and the words came more freely. The next three songs passed in this manner, and though I was relieved to hear Keaton finally call out to the crowd for payment, I also felt a little pleased with myself.

I sang every note!

With shaking legs, I stepped away from my perch and came down the four steps from the stage, wishing for a handrail. Moving behind the cart, I lifted the hat from my head and shook my hair loose.

"Ah ha!" a voice said behind me. "I told you 'twas a girl singing in that guise!"

Turning my head, I saw two boys, likely a little younger than me standing nearby, their arms crossed, squinting at me.

Shyly, I smiled and said, "You've found me out."

"Good god! What's that upon her face?" the first boy sputtered, his eyes wide. "I saw the squattie at first, but *this*, too?"

Galled at this, I winced as the other ass began to laugh uproariously, grabbing ahold of his friend's shoulder as if to keep from falling down.

Dunderheads!

With my face aflame, I opened my mouth though no apt words waited upon my tongue.

Brom hopped off the stage to stand before the boys, towering over them. "Get back to your pen, piglets, afore I make you squeal."

With another smirking glance at me, the boys turned away and strolled off, soon lost amongst the crowd.

"We get some o' that at times," Brom said, lifting his waterskin from a peg on the top step. He took a swig, then wiped his mouth and held it out to me. "Ya done well. I could hear ya."

"Thank you," I murmured faintly, shaking my head at his offer, and anxiously donned the hat again.

"Brom!" a friendly voice hollered.

Peering past the dipping brim, I saw a wiry man with a pointy beard bound over and slap the juggler on his back.

"Marvin!"

"I wondered when we'd run into you!" Marvin turned and hollered, "Hey, Mavis! Look who I've found!"

Within seconds, a dark-haired woman stepped into view. She looked as if she wore a costume as well, though hers was alluring while mine was rough and ragged. The bodice of her dress was tied tightly across the front, looking like poultry trussings, and there were several different colored ribbons braided into her glossy dark hair.

"Ah, Brom," she said, her voice raspy. "I didn't recognize you without your balls in your hands."

"Ha ha ha!" Brom burst out.

Her crude jibe didn't amuse me, but I smiled never having heard Brom laugh in this manner before. I was glad to hear it though I felt embarrassed for him at how oafish and childlike it sounded.

"Who's this?" Mavis asked, turning to look at me.

I froze.

"Ah, that's Madge," Brom said, waving his hand at me dismissively.

I bobbed my head, knowing I should remove my hat as was proper for all introductions, but after a quick glance at me, neither Marvin nor Mavis showed me any more interest. For once I was thankful for Brom's rudeness.

"We had the stage earlier and earned plenty for some ale. Care to join us at the Cackling Hen for a round? Or two or three?" Marvin laughed.

Hmm. What do they *do upon the stage?*

"'Course I will," Brom said.

"And you, Madge," Marvin asked, pulling his beard into a sharper point. "You're welcome, as well."

That was not expected!

"Oh…" I stuttered. "Oh, nay, but I thank you."

"Very well," he shrugged.

Mavis looked me up and down again and announced, "She's got to stay and scare off the crows and rooks that flock about the stage."

I chuckled uncomfortably, hating the sound of it in my ears, glad when they all seemed to forget about me again.

"Oughtn't we to invite dear little Keaton, as well?" Mavis asked, linking her arm through Brom's.

"Nah," Brom said, already walking away, then called over his shoulder to me, "Tell Keaton to put my portion aside and I'll meet ya both later tonight at the place we camped last year."

I watched as Brom disappeared into the crowd. Mavis clung to him, her hips swaying back and forth more than seemed natural. Marvin strode along beside them, talking loudly and gesturing widely with his arms.

I stood, asking myself if I liked Brom's friends or not when I heard Keaton tromping down the stage steps to stand on the ground beside me.

"So off he goes with Delilah and her brother."

"Delilah?" I said. "The man called her 'Mavis'."

"Hmph." Keaton responded. "Well, 'Delilah' fits her a bit better in my mind."

"Who are they, Keaton?"

"Marvin is a fiddler, and a very good one at that. His sister sings a bit, but her true talent is dancing. Truth be told, 'tis hard to keep one's feet still when Marvin's drawing a bow across those strings. But listen to *this*..."

He shook his upturned hat happily, a jangling sound filling my ears.

"*That* sound might make one dance!" he said, bobbing around on his gangly legs. "*And* I heard your voice throughout, Madge the Melodious. Well done, indeed!"

I thought to mention the rude boys who had sullied my joy, but instead I just thanked him.

Brom might tell him later that he was called 'squattie', but that won't be coming from my mouth.

"Let us go somewhere safe to count this out, and I shall happily lay some of it – well earned – into *your* hand, m'lady."

Igniting a Flame

How does Brom do this so quickly?

He was still not returned to us as we set up camp that evening.

"We oughtn't expect him here before dawn," Keaton had said.

I would have been pleased with this news had it not meant *I* must try to light the fire. Keaton had left his fire kit with me before going to a nearby farm to buy something for our supper. Determined to prove my worth as a traveling companion, I wanted to have the flames knee high before he returned.

I've spent most of my life in a kitchen – why can I not light a damned fire? I struck the steel again.

Daylight was dimming around me and I dreaded the thought of being alone in the dark, though I was not entirely alone, as a few other travelers made their way past me on the road now and again. One small group had even set up camp a stone's throw away. Their fire burned already and the smell of roast meat wafted toward me on the evening breeze.

My hands ached from gripping the steel and two of my knuckles were bleeding from being scraped and bashed. As I stood up from a crouch to stretch my back, I yelped, dropping the steel and the stone.

A ghost?

Though I'd never believed in them before, I couldn't help it now as I saw a lone figure standing silently in the gloaming, ten feet away. There was the pale oval of a face, edged by a dark hood, and two white hands emerging from a cloak to drift at waist height. How long it had been there, I had no idea as I had heard no footsteps.

"I did not mean to frighten thee," a woman's voice said.

Is that not a specter's purpose? I wondered, my heart pounding in my throat.

"I will help thee if thou will allow it." She moved forward, and I stepped back as she squatted, throwing the hang of her cloak over her shoulder, to pick up the fallen items.

"Thy char-cloth is damp. 'Twill never ignite in this state." The practical nature of these remarks surprised me.

I watched how her fingers deftly handled the striking kit.

I believe she is *real. No haunting spirit would help to light a fire.*

"See here?" She turned to look up at me and her hand, warm and firm, grasped mine, pulling me down into a crouch. "Thy tinder is too thick. It has the girth of kindling."

Thy? Thee? She speaks as Shakespeare and Milton wrote.

Within moments, the young woman had built a loosely bundled nest of tinder and lit it, then fed little sticks to its flames, speaking helpful bits of advice to me throughout.

"There. Now thou know it," she said, satisfied.

"Yes." I admired the flaming tongues leaping up into the air, warming our faces. "I thank you, truly."

"'Tis but a small favor," she responded, then scooped a handful of dirt over the top of the fire, extinguishing it.

I was aghast, my fear fully spent at such waste. "But why did you...?"

"Thou must try. A lesson spoken is of no use if it remains unlearned. I will help thee. There is still daylight enough to see what is in thy hands. Now first, build a nest of tinder."

I bit my tongue and scraped the forest floor for the driest and lightest of litter, my split knuckles stinging angrily. Balling it up just as the woman had modeled, I dropped a square of char-cloth atop it. Then, following each of her spoken instructions, I soon had a tiny fire of my own burning before me. I gazed at it with a sense of pride though I doubted I could easily repeat it all without her guidance.

"Well done, friend," said the woman as she stood and stuck out her right hand. "I am Thrin Applegate. What is thy name?"

It was truly dark now and the light from the tiny fire was just enough to illuminate her round face. Her features looked large by the strange shadows cast from the light glowing up from the ground.

"I am called Madge," I answered clasping her hand before kneeling to feed larger sticks to the flames.

"Please sit," Thrin said, motioning to the fallen log nearby. "How came thee to be here on this night?"

She bids me sit and speak as if I wandered into her campsite rather than she visiting mine?

"Hullo there! Sorry for the delay!" another voice called out from the dark. Keaton stepped into the firelight, a brace of skinned rabbits dangling limply in his hands. "Why Madge, you've got a fire going!"

"Only with much help. Keaton, this is Thrin. Thrin, meet Keaton."

"I am pleased to meet thee," Thrin said.

In the firelight, Keaton's normally merry face suddenly shifted to the most reserved I had yet seen it. It held the politest of smiles, and his voice sounded cool as he bobbed his head and murmured, "And I, you."

"Please join us," Thrin responded, her head held high. "Madge was just going to tell me of herself."

"But I know her tale," Keaton said, grabbing the spit stand from the cart to erect it above the growing flames. "Yours is the mystery that ought be solved. What brings a young woman like yourself out into the woods on an evening such as this?"

He now had skewered the rabbits through and was adjusting their height above the growing fire.

"Each Seventh Day I travel hither that I might attend Meeting on the First Day in Spirely, then back again home in time for the evening milking. This is my usual sleep site though unlike thee, I build my fire yonder." She pointed toward a blackened spot upon the ground behind me.

Each 'Seventh Day'?

I asked, "What sort of meeting are you so eager to attend that you travel thus?"

"'Tis a gathering of all the Friends around and in Spirely and beyond. Yet all are invited, Friends or not."

"Are you not afeared of that which lurks in the woods and along the road as you travel alone. Have you a dagger at the least?" inquired Keaton.

Though he was asking questions that naturally arose in my mind, his manner was nearly accusing. I expected discourtesy from Brom, but from Keaton it puzzled me.

Why does he not like her? True, she is bossy, but there's something more to his wariness than mere irritation.

"Nay." Thrin responded. "The Inward Light has bid me come and will keep me whether I meet with beast or brute."

Keaton smiled wryly in the firelight and shook his head. "Even Christ urged his men to carry swords in their travels, and I doubt 'twas to split apples."

"Trials and tribulations are promised to all of us, yet we are not to cause them for others, as toting weapons is wont to do."

"'Twould be no trial of *your* making to ensure your own safety against those who would do you harm," Keaton retorted.

"I care not to argue with thee, Keaton. I suspect by thy words that thou are familiar with Friends and what we know to be true. Should thou hope to learn more, I invite thee to Meeting on the morrow. Madge, thou ought to come as well."

"This meeting, is it a service in a church?" I asked.

"If thou speak of a steeple-house, then nay. No building is holy. A Meeting is when Friends come together for mutual edification. A field, a forest, or even a street would serve our purposes, as long as we can quiet ourselves and listen to the Inward Light."

"The Inward Light?"

"Yes. 'Tis the voice of Jesus that speaks to all who would hear Him."

I froze in place.

She hears the voice of God? They all *hear Him?*

"We are not long for this place," Keaton spoke up, still turning the rabbits, clearly unaware of the bolt that had just struck my heart. "Tomorrow we must sing at Spirely's market."

My mouth felt dry as I opened it to speak.

"Surely, we can tarry here a little while, Keaton."

The face he turned to me in the firelight was at first surprised, then troubled and questioning. "What?"

"I...I should very much like to attend this meeting of which she speaks."

Keaton's mouth opened, then shut into a thin, hard line, matched by his lowering brow.

"Madge, I...that is, 'tis not the place for you nor me."

"Keaton," I began, lowering my voice though I knew Thrin would still hear every word. "You know why I followed you out of Trivington, why I am here now alongside this road. Yet, I haven't told you all...but believe me that perhaps this meeting shall help to mend my heart."

"Oh, indeed!" Thrin declared. "Hearts are mended every First Day at Meeting!"

An awkward silence followed, until Thrin went on to offer, "I can remove myself should the two of ye like to speak alone."

"Nay," Keaton said flatly as he stared hard at me. "Stay, Thrin. I've no qualm with you hearing my gripe.

"Madge, I have traveled far and wide. I know what you do not seem to. I mean no disrespect when I tell you that Thrin and her kind call themselves 'Friends' but by some are called 'Fanatiques' and by others 'Quakers'. There are many who would do – nay, many who *do* do them wrong, great wrong. The mildest form being tossing rotten eggs into the midst of their meetings. Far worse, they are at times locked up in gaol simply for not doffing their hats before their superiors. I've even heard tell of a Quaker being ripped limb from limb for *heresy*. Should you be amongst them when an offended party descends upon them, you might find yourself counted as one of these 'Friends', thence gaoled or injured."

Wondering at Keaton's words, I glanced at Thrin whose face was serene. She crouched by the fire and had begun turning the spit's handle, abandoned by Keaton during his speech.

Danger or no, she hears God speak and promises others do as well!

I inhaled deeply.

"Your concern for me is genuine, Keaton, I know, and I understand if you need to go into Spirely tomorrow without me, but I *must* go with her."

Keaton's face fell into such dismay that he looked like a different person.

"Please trust me in this," I said. "I promise I shall flee at the approach of anyone who looks bent on harming us."

Looking more miserable than I had yet seen him, Keaton turned away and stared into the fire. There was silence as Thrin continued to turn the spit until the rabbits were brown and crackling, and it continued even as Keaton motioned to Thrin that she might partake in the eating of them.

In turn, Thrin produced a packet of bread from her sack and wordlessly offered some to both of us. Moments later, when the food was all but eaten, Thrin smiled placidly and murmured almost as if to herself, "The Light said I would not go hungry this evening."

God assured her of such?

A hundred questions for Thrin flooded my mind, but I held my tongue, suspecting the asking would only irk or sadden Keaton. Wondering if we would spend the entire evening in this dark unease, I was relieved to see him retrieve his lute.

"We ought to practice a bit, Madge," he said, joylessly, returning to his spot.

I noted how upright and stiff Thrin looked sitting by the fire, her hands hooked around her knees, her back as straight as a fire iron.

Perhaps the beauty of his music shall salve her and they will become friends.

Clearing my throat, I prepared myself to watch Thrin's face in the firelight for little signs of appreciation. There were none throughout our first song. The group camping nearby cheered happily at its end, which drew neither a smile nor word from Keaton.

"Nicely done, Madge," Keaton said after the third song, and I suddenly realized that I had sung everything within Thrin's hearing without shyness.

My want for them to like each other overrode it, I suppose, but that failed. Her foot did not tap once!

Without another word, Keaton wrapped the lute in its cover and put it away before laying down upon his mat to sleep.

Knowing I had disappointed my one friend in the world, saddened me, but I knew I could do nothing differently.

Seeking God's direction was why I left home! I can't forego the chance this Meeting may offer.

My insides were aflutter at the thought, and I was anxious for the dark hours of the night to pass.

Murmuring a good night to Thrin – which seemed to go unanswered – I laid down, bundling myself in my blanket. Soon, she too, readied herself for sleep on the far side of the fire.

Have You brought me here to the woods on this evening to meet Thrin that I may learn to hear You?

I lay upon the hard ground, gazing past tree branches into the immense and starry sky, longing for a response.

None came.

Well, though You are silent, I see Your Hand in all of this. Please, please help Keaton understand as I am beginning to.

Moments later, I heard deep and even breathing just feet away and knew that Keaton was asleep. Comforted, I too, was able to slip into slumber.

Straining to Hear

The next morning, when the sun had just begun to lighten the sky, I awoke to the trilling of birds and rose to fold my blankets.

Across the way, I could see Brom splayed out upon the ground, both of his arms thrown above his head in the abandonment of sleep. His face was turned toward me, his stubbly chin sagging, leaving his mouth agape. I studied his features, deciding reluctantly that they were well-formed, good even.

He is a manly fellow, I thought, approvingly.

What is it that makes a person pleasing to look upon or not? If a nose well performs its task of smelling, is it not a good nose? Yet some noses we regard as shameful for being large or too long. And eyes. Some can entrance a soul with a glance whilst others excite nothing.

One might call Brom 'handsome' if he were always sleeping. 'Tis the words spilling out of his mouth and his vile habits that are his undoing.

What time did he wander back here? I hope he found the rabbit we left on the spit for him. Ah, indeed. That looks like a bit of it stuck between his two front teeth.

I glanced at Keaton, expecting to see his eyes closed and lips slightly parted in slumber. Instead, I saw he was looking at me, a somber look upon his face.

You don't want me to go, but I must, I tried to say with my eyes. *You may understand later. Once I am healed, perhaps I shall tell you all.*

I wanted to urge him to join me and Thrin, as there might be healing for his misshapen body should he entrust himself to this Inward Light. But the memory of his near disgust at Thrin's words the night before kept me silent.

Perhaps you shall see, Keaton. Maybe in time, you too will benefit from this.

The thought of me, unmarked, and Keaton standing well-formed and tall, singing together on stage filled me with joy and I couldn't suppress a smile.

In return, a small, sad smile formed on his own face, lingering there for a moment before he rolled over and adjusted his blanket.

"Eager, are thou?" Thrin whispered across the campsite. "Up with the birds."

Seeing her in the strengthening sunlight, I was struck with how tidy and clean she was. Though she had just awoken after sleeping all night upon the ground, her hair was smooth and in place, her clothes were not rumpled, and her eyes and complexion were bright and shining. Her nose, which had looked rather broad by firelight, had refined itself in sunlight to a nicety.

She would not likely be called 'beautiful', but one might say she is a 'fine-looking girl'.

"Good morning," I responded, pulling a lock of my hair forward.

She may be seeing my mark for the first time this morning, not able to see it last night in the near dark.

"All mornings are good, as God has made them such," Thrin said simply. "Come. Let us begin. We may be early, but 'twill be good to meet with the Friends afore Meeting begins."

After a hasty breakfast of day old bread, I readied my things and dropped them into the cart. Just before we left, Keaton was up and said that he would remain there until I returned.

As he promised this, the hope I felt was tinged with guilt.

Perhaps, my friend, I shall return only to get my belongings and bid you farewell. You have been so kind to me, 'twould be a shame if we were to part in such a manner, yet nothing will waylay me from going wherever God may tell me to go or doing whatever He may tell me to do.

Now, as Thrin and I walked down the path, cresting a hill to view the rolling distance bathed in young, yellow light, I was full of joyful anticipation, not only at what the meeting might hold, but also in coming to know the young woman beside me.

Throughout the years, I'd seen young women walk through the market together, laughing, and throwing each other knowing looks as if they alone could understand and amuse one another. However, as an only child who'd been raised in an inn – few guests traveled with their children – I myself had rarely ever spoken to another girl my age.

"How came you to be called Thrin? I've never before heard the name."

"Two years past, when I came to know the Inward Light, I perceived my given name was too lofty, thus I became 'Thrin', though my mother insists on calling me 'Catherine' still, much to my displeasure. And thou? Have thou always been 'Madge'?"

"No, I was christened *'Margaret'*, though I'm never called it."

"Just as well. Simply 'Madge' will suffice and besides, ceremonies such as christenings are needless, mere attempts to confine God to a place and time."

"My mother was there for it," I said, slightly irritated. Though I couldn't remember it, my christening was precious to me. To know I had been in my mother's arms while the water was poured over my head, reminded me that she hadn't always been only a very faded memory.

"I think thou shall enjoy the simplicity of the Meeting of Friends."

Ah yes, I am soon to meet with many strangers.

"Why preen thee thy hair so often?" Thrin asked.

"What?" I asked, then realized I had just pulled more hair free from the knot at my nape to let it drop in front of my face.

"Thou did several times last night, and now here thou are, tugging and primping anew."

I floundered for an answer, ashamed that she had noticed my attempts to conceal my birthmark.

Though she had asked me a question, Thrin did not wait for a response. "Vanity gains us nothing."

"I'm loosening my locks. A tight knot makes my head to ache."

She either ignored my lie or saw through it, and said, "We live for only a little while. Therefore, we do well to be prudent and wise in all of our actions, great and small."

Recognizing truth in this, but still riled, I said nothing and tried not to touch my tresses again. The keenness I'd just felt for this new friendship began to wane.

"I know vanity well," Thrin continued. "Before I heeded the Inward Light, I loved to wear a rose-colored gown my mother had made for me."

I eyed the dark blue gown and cloak she now wore and asked, "Why would you not don it still?"

"The levity such a gown brought to my heart was improper." Casting me a shamed glance, she lowered her voice and admitted, "I would oft gaze upon myself in the looking glass, turning this way and that to see it from every side."

She scoffed, then shook her head and declared, "Our hearts are for God's inhabitation, not for flighty, shifting fancies. Hair arrangments, clothing, music, dancing – all of these will distract us from our higher purpose if we take no heed."

Thus why she was so unmoved by our songs last night, I realized. *Are all Quakers this dour?*

With every step we took closer to Meeting, I felt more anxious.

"But what's to make our days merry if not the levity you seem to scorn?" I dared to ask.

Her answer was dealt more quickly than I expected.

"Why, doing good deeds, of course, and regarding the beauty that God Himself has made. See here before thee? The hills are aglow with morning light." She spread out her arms toward the horizon, and breathed in deeply, ending with a contented sigh.

'Tis a beautiful day, I conceded, gazing out at the rolling, tree-topped hillocks and barrows around us. A light mist hung in their hollows. *And God made it*

all...yet He also made my throat to sing and Keaton's feet to dance, no matter how clumsy!

These thoughts I kept to myself, sensing more and more clearly that gainsaying Thrin was useless.

Is it the Inward Light that so emboldens her tongue and mind, or merely her own stubborn spirit?

This question troubled me as I considered how I might be altered if *I* was to hear God as clearly as Thrin said she did.

I dread the thought of irking others at each opening of my mouth. And 'twould feel so unnatural upon my tongue to 'thee' and 'thou' all who are near.

"Come!" Thrin said suddenly, surprising me by grabbing my hand. "I am so pleased that thou shall meet the Friends. Good people are they, devout and modest."

The smile she wore made her look quite happy, pretty even, and I forced myself to smile back, feeling the odd sensation of her hand clutching my own, and wondering at the traits she seemed to cherish most in her people.

'Devout and modest'? If I were to become one of them, could I be seen as such? Modest, perhaps, but devoted? I could feign such perhaps before people, but God is fooled by no one.

Yet, if doing so would cleanse my face and You wanted it of me, I would try. Truly, God, I would try as well as I could.

"Thou look troubled, Madge." Thrin said, swinging our joined hands between us. "Are thou wary?"

Unwilling to reveal my thoughts entirely, I faltered, then said, "I am never at ease in the company of even one stranger, and here we go to meet many."

"Why is such a trial for thee?"

If I tell you of my shame over my mark, you will likely charge me again with vanity!

I simply stated, "I've been shy since I was a wee one."

"Thou needn't be. Thou speak well and thy heart is good. Yet even if 'twere not so, none should be shy as all were made by God in His image and therefore are altogether equal."

Ugh! Will you not let me feel what I feel? And why must you give your opinion on nearly everything?

"Hmm," I murmured, disliking more and more the weight of her hand in my own.

Was it only a few moments ago that I was hoping to talk and giggle with her like two milkmaids heading out to the barn together? 'Tis impossible to be at ease with someone who studies and corrects not only one's words but even one's pulling of a lock of hair.

Coming around a curve in the road, I saw nearby a building, plain and stout. By its door stood many people, all dressed in clothing as drab as Thrin's. Some looked at us and waved, smiling. Smaller groups of people were approaching the building from the road and across fields behind it. One couple fell into place behind us, and with quick strides were closing the gap between.

"Lower not thy head," Thrin urged me. "Hold it high, not in pride of thyself, but because God has made thee and thou are in His service as an agent for good here and wherever else He may send thee."

This chiding was especially carking as it was loud enough for the nearby couple to hear.

Know you nothing of whispering? I hope I find others here amiable, as you are wearing quite thin upon me!

I looked around at the many Friends, trying not to appear as if I was examining them. All looked at me with kindness, some with interest. My mark burned upon my face.

What an odd collection of people!

The group was about thirty souls, milling about, chatting happily. There was something strange about their salutations that at first, I could not fix upon. But then, I knew it.

Every one of the men has kept their hat upon their head. There is no doffing and bowing to betters in this group. And betters there are!

Some were dressed in unadorned but good quality clothes while others appeared as if they had pulled their garments from a rag bag.

One man of the ragged group, hunched forward in the shoulders and shuffling along, caught his toe on a stone in the road. A nearby man caught him in the stumble and the two laughed together.

"I am here for thee, friend," the catcher said.

"I thee that and thank thee," the stubber responded, his words sloppily formed.

I believe he may be short on teeth, I thought, looking at the fellow's jaws.

As if alerted to my interest, the man made his way toward us.

"I greet thee, Thrin," he said, his lips loose and flapping as he turned to look at me.

I tried not to flinch as a drop of spittle hit my cheek.

"And thou hath brought another, I thee. What ith thy name, Friend?"

I squirmed at the greeting.

Do they think I'm one of them?

I was quick and stout in my response.

"I am called Madge. Good morning to you, sir," I said, and bobbed into a little curtsy, a gesture I hadn't seen amongst any of the women.

If he insists that 'all mornings are good', I just may run all the way back to Keaton and Brom. Ha! Imagine preferring Brom's manners over those of another!

It seemed that Thrin shifted uncomfortably beside me, though she remained silent.

See there, Thrin, I am not one of you, only a curious girl who likes to sing and bid others' good day', with nary a 'thee' nor a 'thou' upon my lips. Though your people seem kind generally, I am thus far not convinced of the need to embrace your ways, nor your beliefs.

"I am pleathed to meet thee, Madge. I am called Lyle," the man continued.

"And I, you," I responded.

Though it was at no one's urging, the crowd started to thin as people made their way into the building.

"Now, we shall wait in the Light," Thrin said, her face suddenly lit with a rapturous smile. I followed her up the steps and through the door. Once inside, I paused a moment to look around.

The room was large and plain. No curtains hung on the windows, and the few candles present were ensconced upon plain, wooden stands. The walls were flanked with rows of roughly-hewn benches, all facing inward to the room's center where there was neither a stage nor a pulpit.

But where does the choir sit? Oh, of course! They have no choir as music is 'useless levity'.

141

There were two fireplaces, one on each side, both open wide that their cavernous, soot-coated bellies yawned at all who entered.

And in winter, does Thrin chide the flames for dancing about within the fireplaces?

I hoped to remember this joke to share with Keaton as I continued my observance. Several people had already sat down. Seeing that Thrin was one of them, I moved to get the place beside her as more people came in. The jovial sounds of those still outdoors abruptly halted at the door, laughter and words dying suddenly upon their lips. In they came, heads bowed, hands folded before them, making their way steadily to the benches around the room.

As the place filled, I wished Thrin had sat two rows back, against the wall rather than so near the room's center. Where we sat, many eyes could peer at me while I felt so out of place.

And yet, no one is doing so. Those ladies there are quietly studying their hands in their laps. And he has shut his eyes altogether.

A young woman, seated and holding a swaddled bundle in her arms, caught my eye. While the others looked reverent in their solemnity, she appeared grave, all her features lax and still.

The thought that I was watching others to see if they watched me, made me lower my eyes.

I shall wait until the priest arrives. Surely 'tis acceptable to look upon him *as he speaks. Yet, which way will he face as he stands in the center there. Does he tread on the toes of those in front? Everyone is in now, are they not? Where is the man?*

The last person entering had shut the door behind him and a stillness, heavy and deep, settled on the room. The quiet of the now near fifty people was so complete that I could hear a gentle buzzing deep within my ears. A long moment passed, interrupted only by the occasional sound of a woman sniffing.

How shameful their leader is tardy! Or was he dragged off to gaol on his way here? Is no one concerned?

The sniffling continued.

Ugh. I wish the Inward Light would tell her 'Blow thy nose, for 'tis better to jar thy neighbors with one mighty blast than to needle them with thy ever sniveling.'"

Yet more silence, and then, a woman rose from her seat and cleared her throat as if to say something.

A woman *will speak in church? This is new!*

No heads turned toward her. No eyes lifted. It was as if no one noticed her except for me. But then, she said, "The Inward Light has urged me to think more on the plight of our Friends imprisoned in London, but not *just* think. I have determined to go there on this week's Third Day and take them blankets for their comfort and anything that any of ye is wont to give. Of course, company on this venture would be very much appreciated."

With that she sat down. A barely perceptible movement of a few heads nodding slightly was all the acknowledgement her words received.

Suddenly, the door opened, and I turned my head to see the priest's entrance.

He is here at last!

However, it was no man. The door had opened just wide enough to admit a small, elderly woman. She tottered with a cane, clunking across the wooden floor to a bench onto which she lowered herself.

I bit my lips to hinder a smile. *Well, that is certainly not him.*

The silence renewed, it stretched on and on until I could barely keep from squirming. The stomach of someone near me rumbled.

I am ready to leave these strange, quiet people. If I wanted such silence, I could wander into the woods alone. Where is this Inward Light?

Just as I dreamed of departure, Lyle the Toothless, who was a few places to my left, rose. He wiped his mouth solemnly and then began to speak.

"I believe I mutht remind uth all that ath the Book of Hebrewth thez, without faith 'tith impothible to pleathe God: for he that cometh to God mutht believe that He ith, and that He ith a rewarder of them that diligently theek Him."

Having been to church often in Trivington, this phrase was not unfamiliar to me. But bits of it struck me anew as Lyle lowered himself to his seat.

'Tis in Scripture that God's true nature is revealed. '...a rewarder of them that diligently seek...'

I *am diligently seeking. Will He reward* me?

And what of the first part? 'Without faith, 'tis impossible to please God.'

But what is *faith?*

The silence in my head at this question felt more immense than the quietude of the entire meeting house. It yawned at me from within myself. I was only able to push it aside when a man with broad shoulders stood and cleared his throat.

"I am shamed to say I could not understand why Wee Thomas was born without a left thumb. 'Twould be a trial for any blacksmith bent on teaching his son to ply the trade, but God knew that and wrought him as He did.

"I hereby repent before ye of my grief over it." He sighed heavily, as though the telling tired him, and motioned to the woman sitting beside him. It was the woman I had noticed earlier holding a baby close to her chest. "Lucilla and I both do."

A glance at Lucilla's face, made me doubt she was equally penitent as her husband. Etched on her features was a melancholy so pure that there was no room there for any other emotion. A single tear slipped down her cheek as she adjusted her hold on the wrapped infant.

I saw that no one else witnessed Lucilla's unmistakable grief as every eye was downturned.

Have pain and sadness no value here?

Perhaps they are granting her privacy for such. You don't want to cry before others.

"Yet, this week I have read in John's gospel," the man continued. "Jesus was asked, 'Why was this man born blind?' to which He replied, '…that the works of God should be manifested in him.' Then He plastered mud over the man's eyes and told him to go wash in the waters."

This was a story I'd not heard before.

"The man returned seeing and many gave glory to God because of it."

The waters healed him? My heart felt as if it had skipped a beat. *Is this the Inward Light speaking to me?*

The smithy spoke on, and I strained to hear any more striking notes in his words.

"Believing the works of God trump all, even our own desires, we pray that much good would come of Wee Thomas' left hand. I ask – *we* ask – that ye would keep us in the Light in this matter." He abruptly sat down and put his arm around Lucilla, drawing her and the baby closer to himself as the great silence of the room returned.

So waters, should they be holy, could heal me?

Without faith, 'tis impossible to please God, so said Sir Toothless. Yet, how can I force *myself to believe something strongly enough to please Him?*

A woman stood, but I heard her not as I wrestled with my thoughts.

Is it merely a matter of determining such? That is how it sounds!

Very well, God, I hereby resolve in faith that taking the waters at Tersewell will heal me of this mark. Does that please You?

Silence.

Did that seem glib, God? Please forgive me if it did as I didn't mean it to.

Something in the air of the meeting house began to feel restless and soon some Friends rose and made their way out the door. The room was half empty when Thrin herself stood and left, and I was pleased to follow her as my mind was disquieted and my backside was numb.

"Thrin and Madge, will ye not join uth for a breaking of bread and time of fellowthip?" Lyle inquired. Most of the people had already laid out blankets and were sitting upon them with open baskets of food beside them.

Please say nay, Thrin!

I needed quiet to think through what I had just learned without feigning pleasure at talking with strangers.

"We thank thee, Lyle, but I must start back that I might reach home before dark," Thrin said. "And Madge's companions are expecting her. I have cheese and bread in my sack that we will not hunger."

"Very well," the man said, nodding with a smile. "Far be it from me to thtand in the way of thothe bent on diligenth. I hope to thee both of ye at nektht Meeting. Go in the Light."

Others in the group raised their hands to us, bidding us to depart in peace.

My uneasy thoughts kept me from doing so.

Disappointing Thrin

The hills were now bright under the noonday sun, the mist having burned off while we were at Meeting.

Thrin, stepping along beside me, had hooked her hand through the crook of my elbow as we made our way back to the campsite. It was she who had invited and taken me to Meeting, so I forbore the urge to disentangle myself from her though the pull of her hand nettled me.

Who is to say that I am to be healed? Scripture was writ long ago, and neither my name nor my mark are in it.

Ugh! Such fickle thoughts! If my faith for healing is strong enough, then it may please God to do it...

"Well?" Thrin asked.

I must get to Tersewell. Could I go on without *Keaton? He is determined to stop and sing every chance he gets.*

"Hmm?" I murmured.

Nay. I know not the way.

"What did thou think of Meeting?"

But I know 'tis near Thorneby. When we get to Wexhall, I could take a coach from there and ask around about the abbey ruins...

"Madge?"

"Oh. Umm, 'twas very different than I expected. Why was there no priest?"

"*Priest!*" Thrin said the word with amused disdain. "We have no *priest*! We have the Inward Light. Did He not speak to thee?"

What am I to say? She'll likely pick it all apart and prove that she knows all and I know naught.

Nay! 'Tis not fair to think thus. She hears God so often – every day it seems. Perhaps she can help discern the message.

"Well, I…I *think* He did." I scrambled for an answer, hesitant to share with her all I was thinking. "I know that without faith 'tis impossible to please God."

Tightening her grip on my elbow, Thrin halted, pulling me to a stop as well.

"Thy eyes have been opened!" she said in quite a different voice. "Oh, this gladdens me so!"

Most coaches leave at dawn, but perhaps I could catch one that's stopped to change horses at noon…

"The Truth has been planted in thy heart!" she went on, her eyes aglow. "But, how can we allow it to take root properly? Oh, I know! Thou may come home with me and offer my parents help with the farm work. There is always so much to do that they shall be glad of it."

"Hmm?" I asked, confused.

"There is plenty of food as of late, so they will not begrudge thee thy meals, and I shall share my bed with thee, so thou won't require a room of thy own."

"Thrin, I've no ambition to…I mean…"

"Oh, but one thing I ask of thee…" she interrupted and said, as though somewhat embarrassed. "Do not share with them thy new convictions."

"What mean you?"

"Well, I know we ought to share our beliefs amply that others may hear and believe, but my parents are displeased that I have become a Friend and would likely turn their noses up at thee should thou confess having done the same."

Oh, nay! Nay! I am no 'Friend'!

"We shall tell them that I met thee on the road and that thou are in need of work. That is true, is it not?"

"Thrin," I began gently. "You seem to misunderstand me. That is…"

Unable to look her in the eye, I squeezed her arm against my side and started to walk again, propelling her along.

"I am not quite ready to…to become a Friend."

"But, Madge," Thrin replied, patiently. "If the Light spoke to thee of faith, He could mean none other than the true one! I urge thee to pray and listen more closely."

I stifled a groan of frustration.

I have *prayed and I* have *listened, Thrin. Now if* you *would just* listen to me *without scolding, then perhaps you would understand. I must get to* Tersewell, *not to Applegate Farm!*

Taking a breath, I said, "Thrin, there may come a time that I will join you and the other Friends, but for now, I know that I must continue on with Keaton and then return home to my father. *That* is what the Light told me this morning."

There! She will have to respect that as she wouldn't dare gainsay the 'Inward Light'.

But it was not so. Solemnly, Thrin released my arm and announced with a sniff, "I trust the Light would make it known to thee if thou would but seek Him with thy *whole* heart."

Then she fell quiet and seemed set on remaining that way.

My whole *heart? How could I possibly be more sincere in my seeking? Yes, Thrin, sulk in silence. 'Twill be a joy to witness and give me a moment to think.*

God? Was my confession to her full of enough faith? Believing that You spoke to me this morning through Scripture and the words of others, I hereby promise to continue on to Tersewell at whatever pace I am allowed.

The silence continued as we drew nearer the campsite.

* * *

When Thrin and I returned, both men had been busy with tasks. Keaton paused while organizing the contents of one of his baskets to murmur a hello, and Brom didn't even look up as he sharpened his dagger on a strap.

Thrin lingered at the campsite only long enough to refill her flask with water from the stream, then took her leave, saying with a stiff smile on her face, "Madge, I hope that thou will seek the Inward Light with purity of heart henceforth. Perhaps we shall meet again someday."

"Yes, Thrin." I smiled brightly, determined to show her I felt no shame at her grudge. "I am glad to have met you. Thank you for helping me make fire last night and for inviting me today."

"All are welcome at Meeting," she said with a little shrug, as if the invitation had been obvious, then started out at a purposeful pace down the road.

Ugh. She'll likely pull the cows' teats too hard at milking tonight, poor things. Is there anyone she confides in? Laughs with? I think to be so pious is to be utterly alone.

Once she disappeared around the corner, Keaton stowed his basket within the cart and asked, "Ready?"

"Yes," I said, smiling wryly at him, which did not draw him into inquiry as I thought it would.

His face remained placid, uncurious.

The loneliness I felt at this was blunted by the knowledge that once we were on the road, we'd be drawing closer to Tersewell.

Not a word was said for the first hour of our journey.

Later, he shall ask, I reasoned. *Perhaps I ought to tell him tonight of my aim to get to Tersewell, though he may think me foolish.*

Surely, he sees that I've not turned Quaker. That ought to relieve him some.

I thought back on the people I had met that day. They were a curious group. There was the blacksmith who bared his heart to all in the meeting house, and his sad wife beside him, clutching her one-thumbed baby. There was also Sir Lyle Toothless, likeable in spite of his spraying spittle.

Not all were as pious and vexing as Thrin. In fact, none seemed to be so. I must have met at first with the most trying of them all.

Had You told me to join their sect, God, I would have, but You remained silent, as You always seem to.

A swell of guilt filled my chest at that last accusing thought.

But God was not *silent. There was the story of the blind man. True, 'twas not a voice as before – well, 'twas the voice of a smithy, rather – but by faith, I trust it as a message from Him.*

But if you truly have faith, why would you not *tell Keaton of your newly honed purpose? It matters not what he thinks of it, but only what faith you yourself have in it.*

My head began to ache with confusion as I stepped, one foot before the other.

'Twill all make sense once I'm at Tersewell.

Finally, as the first hour stretched into the second, I could stomach the silence no longer.

Will we say nothing? It seems I *must begin it.*

"What thought you of Thrin?" I fished.

The question was aimed at Keaton, but Brom snorted, scoffingly. "Don't fancy wenches plain and prudey such as that."

Recalling Thrin's fresh, pink and white complexion so striking against the dark of her hood, and later the way the sun had glinted off the reddish highlights in her hair, I said, "Plain? I thought her fair enough…in looks anywise."

"Hmph! She prob'ly shushed the birds all the way home."

Such an apt word from the mouth of Brom brought quick and easy laughter to my lips. "But the two of you spoke not at all! You hardly saw her!"

"'Twas long enough. I saw what she was soon as she marched in, lookin' down her nose at ev'rythin'."

He didn't even hear the things she said on the way to Meeting, and yet her nature was so plain to someone as doltish as him?

Keaton chuckled, then looked up into the trees and said in an airy, feminine voice, "Thy levity of heart provokes God to envy. Frown more that He may smile."

"That is rather severe," I said, though snickering. "What think you of her claims of hearing God's voice?"

"Methinks rather, she believes *her own* voice to be that of God," Keaton said.

"Think you not that God may speak to anyone He wills?"

The minstrel was silent for a moment, finally saying, "Aye. Yet the people who claim most often to hear from Him seem to have the dullest ears of all.

"Think of that fellow who demanded I change my song. Men like him have entered churches – I've walked through some of them – and smashed everything of beauty all in the name of God's will. *They* are the superstitious ones – thinking a lovely sight can beguile men for evil as if beauty were the stink eye of a witch!

"Why are the pious so wary of beauty?" he continued. "Does not all beauty, whether in nature or of our doing, have its beginning in Him?"

I nodded slowly.

"And they always go on 'bout not lookin' at wenches. 'Tisn't possible!" Brom muttered.

But what of me? Is my aim to be rid of this marring badge on my face moored in pride?

Nay. I long not for vain beauty, but simply to not feel shame whilst facing my father.

Having said their piece, the others continued the subject no further. I walked on, glad that they could not hear the turmoil roiling in my head.

Why do desires stir up such guilt? Ought I not want what most have by nature—a face free of marks?

Looking out over the fields we were slowly passing, I felt such weight upon my chest.

How long for Tersewell?

The Kiss

The village's strange people were all around us, sitting in the shade of the trees, some stretching out there for a midday nap after having finished their dinner. Their appearance was not what made me pause and study them, as their clothing and faces looked like any others we had seen in the towns and villages where we had sung. They had been pleased to hear us as we stood in their midst singing, even dancing at times. Then they clapped for Brom as his beanbags arced above their heads up into the bright blue summer sky.

"Who are these people, Keaton?" I asked, watching as a villager tore a hunk of bread off of a long, thin loaf offered to him by a smiling woman. "I understand not a word they speak."

"Come," he replied. "Let's go down to the stream there and I'll tell you."

Off to our right, down a grassy knoll was a brook, sparkling in the sunlight. Busking in the sun, with my scarecrow hat pulled low over my face had left me sweating from heat and nervousness. Slightly aswoon, I longed to dip my feet in the running water.

We made toward it, leaving Dame and Brom, dozing already in the shade of the cart.

"They are come from France," Keaton said.

Ah! So that *is the sound of the French tongue.*

"How do a group of French have their own village here in England?" I asked.

"I believe they were driven from their homes, reviled for their beliefs and came across the Channel to settle here," Keaton said.

So they are like the Quakers of whom you are so wary? My mind flickered, but I said naught of it. Any frustration he'd felt at my attending the Friends' meeting the day before, seemed to have dissolved completely and I wanted nothing to revive it.

"They paid a fair amount," he said, jangling a few coins in his breeches' pocket. "It went quite well, don't you think?"

"I feel I sang fairly well, if that's what you mean," I responded, looking back up the hill to see if anyone was nearby. Seeing no one, I doffed my hat.

"It seems singing is getting much easier for you."

Realizing I had just sung before a crowd of thirty or so without my voice even once squeaking or fading into uneasy murmurs, I replied, "Aye."

My answer was honest, but the sentiment seemed trifling as we drew closer to the stream and my mind wandered elsewhere.

It's been three days since I left home. Pappy will have returned by now and know that I've gone.

I imagined him coming inside after stabling Fleet, his arms full of sample wines, expecting to see me hard at work in the kitchen. He and Babs would talk and soon realize that I had *not* been with the other during the previous days as they had both supposed.

I grew queasy as my mind's eye saw him next running up to my room to search for me, then frantically rush around the grounds for any clue of my whereabouts, eventually finding the note I'd left in the guest ledger.

What did I write? 'I am safe and will return when I am able'? That *will be but little consolation.*

I will come home to you, Pappy! But I must be healed first that you can look on me without pain.

We reached the brook and I sat on a large stone to remove my shoes.

And with enough faith, I shall be.

Keaton sat down beside me.

"I don't mean to frighten you, but Wexhall is quite populous. Which is good as I made a lot of money there last year. But I thought busking here in Vraimont – a small, friendly village – before going into Wexhall tomorrow would help put you at ease. And now, look! You're doing so well, it oughtn't be a problem."

He is always thinking of my good, and I cannot ease Pappy's mind from here…unless I was to post a letter…

This fresh notion heartened me and I turned to Keaton, smiling. "'Twas thoughtful of you."

"Oh, look! A little armored friend!" Keaton pointed.

Just above our heads, there was a four-legged creature, sunning itself on a tree branch. The color of common dirt, it was about the length of my hand, and covered in scales.

Keaton reached for it, panicking the lizard which fell to the ground, belly up. Its underside was a flash of bright orange. Righting itself with a heave of its tail, it was suddenly gone, lost amongst the streamside rocks and mud.

"I meant you no harm!" Keaton called after it, then said, "He was perched there as still as a stone, but at sight of my hand, he fled as if I'd said I'd slice him through. Where do you suppose they go at night?"

"Don't know," I shrugged, my mind drifting back to Pappy.

"I've always wondered. They warm themselves in the sun, but what do they do once it sets?" Keaton tilted his head. "Perhaps there's a little inn somewhere, a Gander's Wing of sorts, if you will, where a whole family of them cuddle up together at night. *Or* maybe they all run their separate ways to hide and shiver alone until dawn."

He laughed, turning to look at me.

Oh, Pappy!

I forced a little laugh, though my heart ached.

"Is something wrong, Madge?" Keaton's face fell. "Oh, you're missing your family, aren't you? I'm sorry I said that."

There was such concern in his face that I opened my mouth to assure him somehow, but I paused, thinking.

Ought I to tell him now, about Tersewell? Maybe he'll take me there straight away and I can get home sooner.

Nay. I can't have my only friend in all the world think me a fool!

But if your faith is strong enough, it oughtn't matter what he thinks.

A rustling of leaves behind us arrested his attention. We both turned to look.

A little girl had descended the hillside and was approaching us, lifting the hem of her skirt delicately, revealing bare feet as she stepped across the ground. She looked to be about seven years old and her dark hair was pulled back with a pink ribbon, sloppily tied into a bow. She smiled, shyly glancing again and again at us as she drew ever closer.

"It seems we have a new friend," Keaton said, happily. "One that does *not* flee from us. Bon jour, mademoiselle!'

"Bon jour, monsieur," responded her quiet, gentle voice. "Et vous, madamoiselle."

I resisted the urge to clap my hat back on my head, though I did not lift my face as I murmured a response.

'Tis only a little girl, I chided myself. *And an unshod, friendly one, at that.*

"Voulez-vous des cerises?" she asked, holding her hand out to us.

Resting on her upturned palm were a few pinkish cherries. Though they looked as if they had been picked far too early, I was touched by the sweet charity of her childish heart.

I suppose I ought to take one and smile through its tartness.

Facing her fully, I reached for one of her little offerings. As my fingers scraped her palm, she looked up at me with large, brown eyes.

As if struck by lightning, her face flashed from timid goodwill to surprise, then tensed into something akin to grief. The cherries fell to the ground and her hands flew to her chest as though she meant to steady her heart beneath them. Large tears welled in her eyes though her gaze never wavered from my face. Then, stranger still, she smiled as wide as a rainbow as she continued to stare and weep. It all happened as quickly as the lizard's fall and flight.

"Keaton?" I said, following the word with nothing else. I stared at her face, wondering anxiously what passion would next appear there.

"I see, and understand it not," Keaton said, quietly.

"Lulu!"

A man appeared, hurrying down the knoll toward us. His long legs covered the space quickly and he was soon behind the joyfully weeping child.

"Lulu?" he said, reaching for her.

"Papa." Lulu pointed at me. "Elle est comme Maman!"

The man looked at me and his breath caught in his throat.

"Oui. Je la vois." He picked her up while they both continued to stare at me.

I grew even more uneasy under his gaze.

The ogling of a child is one thing, but that of a grown man is quite another!

"I'd like to go now, Keaton," I whispered, putting the hat back on and reaching for my shoes.

"Non!" Lulu cried out.

"Lulu, silence," the man said, shaking his head apologetically while he stroked the child's hair.

"Please…English there." He beckoned us, motioning toward the top of the hill. His eyes, large and brown like Lulu's, were pleading. "Please come."

"Madge?" Keaton asked. "Shall we join them?"

I shrugged, uneasy. "I suppose we need to climb up there anyway to get back to Dame and Brom."

"Ah, merci," the man said, nodding and smiling as I motioned that I would follow him. "Merci beaucoup!"

Ugh. Why can I not simply vanish? I wondered, donning my shoes.

Once we were atop the knoll, Lulu struggled out of her father's arms to the ground and fell into step beside me. She startled me by slipping her small hand into my own. Her crying had ceased, but her eyes were still wet as she gazed up at me, smiling widely.

Something softened within me.

Her manners are sorely lacking, but she means well, I decided and allowed her little hand to cling to mine though it all felt so very odd.

"Please…come," Lulu's father said again, pointing at a two-story building across the small market square.

"Keaton?" I said with a glance over my shoulder.

"I'm just behind you," he assured.

We entered a dim storeroom with bulging burlap sacks, large enough for a person to climb into, lining the floor against one wall. A row of empty washtubs filled the rooms' center. Against another wall were shelves lined with bottles of various shapes and sizes. Past this all, the Frenchman led us up a staircase.

At its top, we emerged in a large bright room with many tall windows. There were looms everywhere, all heavily strung but still as no one sat at them to work them.

The weavers are those outside under the trees, I supposed.

But in the far corner, was a smaller loom where someone *was* at work. It was an elderly woman, small and hunched in the shoulders. Her feet worked the lower levers of the loom while her hand pushed and pulled with wondrous vigor.

Clack! Foooop. Clack! Foooop.

Lulu's father called out, "Marie! J'ai besoin d'aide!"

The rhythmic sounds of the working loom ceased.

We crossed the floor quickly to all stand beside the little woman who had turned to face us. Peering out of her very wrinkled face was a pair of shiny black eyes. I looked at the floor, avoiding her piercing gaze.

"Qu'est-ce que tu veux, Pierre?" the woman asked in a rattling voice.

In a flurry of French, both Pierre and Lulu began to tell her a drawn-out tale, speaking loudly though they were only four feet from her.

I dared look up and saw that Marie's eyes darted from Lulu to Pierre, to me, then back to Pierre. Her wizened face was puzzled as she opened her mouth to speak, and then vexed as the two prattled on.

"Arretez!" She barked them into silence, then pointed at a well-lit spot on the wooden floor, saying, "Step een-to zee light."

Though I heard the words, it took me a moment to realize what they were and that they'd been said to me. Marie snapped her fingers brusquely and pointed again. Lulu tugged on my arm and suddenly I was there with the warmth of sunlight falling through the window onto my body.

"Take off zee hat!"

Reluctantly, I pushed it off my head to let it hang down my back by its cord.

The woman squinted, her sharp eyes assessing me in a very different way than Lulu's had been earlier. I couldn't help but squirm where I stood and glanced at Keaton who winked at me as he bit his lower lip.

Laugh not, Little Minstrel. You may be next!

Both Pierre and Lulu began to speak hurriedly again.

"Tais-toi!" Marie snapped at them, then spoke to me.

"Zey say you rhe-mind zem of zee girl's muzzer."

"Oh, I…I remind them of her *mother*? Wh-where is her mother now?"

"Zee muzzer died in France before zey fled here. Lulu sez you *look* like her and her fazzer agrees. What eez your name?"

"M-madge," I said. "How do I look like her? Did she have light brown hair?"

Marie looked affronted at my witlessness.

"Not zee hair." She reached up and patted her own cheek. "*Zee red face*! Her muzzer had a beeg spot but on zee right, not zee left."

What? Her mother – his wife – was marked*?*

I felt dizzy, holding tighter to the little girl's hand.

Past Marie, Pierre peered at me, pleased. His eyes, no longer apologetic, were bright above a gentle smile as if to say, 'Now you understand'.

Lulu, too, was beaming up at me, her joy the purest I'd ever seen splashed across a face.

I swayed in the warmth of the sunbeam, thankful when Keaton stepped up beside me and grabbed my other arm.

"And now," Marie declared as her hands settled back onto her loom, "I weave. Go!"

As suddenly as the revelation began, it was over and we were ousted, though my feet didn't move.

Clack! Foooop. Clack! Foooop.

Keaton steered me toward the stairs, and I floated down them, hearing again and again, '*Zee red face! Her muzzer had a beeg spot…*'

Through the storeroom I drifted.

I remember so little of my own mother…

We emerged from the building, back into the bright sun.

…the woman who gave me life…

Standing in the street now, I heard a bell ring, muffled and distant.

…who fed me and held me. Loved me.

The people of Vraimont rose from their spots in the shade, and some filed past me toward the building.

There was a tug on my arm, pulling me down into a crouch and I was face to face with Lulu, inches from her snub nose and darkly fringed eyes.

Your mother is dead, Little One.

And she was marked.

I studied the faint freckles on her nose and her tiny dry lips which were pursed in thought.

We understand each other, you and I, I tried to tell her silently, *we who are motherless and longing.*

But her eyes were not delving into my own. She was gazing at my left cheek.

Seeing my mark brings you joy, a painful joy certainly, but one that you want *to feel.*

Her small hand came up slowly, reaching to push my stray locks aside.

Continuing to kneel steadily before her, a strange willingness overtook me and I turned the left side of my face to her, closing my eyes that she might see every bit of my spot more clearly.

And then, my breath caught in my throat as her finger had touched the birthmark itself and was tracing it carefully, slowly.

No one ever...

I was frozen in place as her gentle touch glided from the corner of my mouth, up along my nose and then above my eye, just under my brow.

I hardly ever touch it myself.

In that blind moment, my eyes welled with tears.

"Votre rose...très belle," Lulu breathed softly, the warmth of her words on my face and throat.

But then, I felt an even stranger sensation, damp and fleeting, upon my cheek.

She kissed me.

It jarred me like a smack on the face.

She kissed me right in the center of my damned, blighting mark.

With my ears buzzing, I rose to a standing position and woodenly patted Lulu on the head, suddenly wanting away from her, no matter how innocent and gentle she was.

"Papa!" She said something to Pierre, smiling, knowing naught of what had just happened inside of me.

He nodded at her words and said to me. "Please…eat…night?"

My eyes burning, I forced myself to watch him as he mimicked eating something with a pretend spoon.

"I believe he's inviting us to supper," Keaton said.

Nay!

"Oh, oh, nay. We couldn't." I shook my head vigorously, untangling my hand from Lulu's grip.

"Madge, we could tarry here a…" Keaton began.

"Nay. We must stay the planned course, get to Wexhall," I insisted.

Get to Tersewell.

There was deep disappointment in Pierre's eyes as I bowed my head at him and said, "But thank you. Thank you very much."

I reached my hand out to him, smiling with a gladness I did not feel, an eerie chuckle sputtering in my throat.

"Merci, mademoiselle," he replied sadly, bowing over my hand and looking as if he would touch his lips to my knuckle.

Having been touched too much already, I cringed, trying not to snatch my hand back from him. Much to my relief, he straightened up, and released me.

Lulu began to cry, neither in the joyous nor thoughtful ways she had done before and reached out for my hand again.

"Good bye, Lulu, sweet girl," I said, pinching her fingers in a quick and awkward handshake.

"Au revoir, Lulu. Pierre." Keaton said, his voice low. He reached to grasp Lulu's hand and held it for a long moment. So long, in fact, that I began to walk away.

"Au revoir...mes amies," the child said, her voice breaking on every word.

The sound of Lulu weeping sickened me and I could no longer hold back my tears. They ran down my face in long, warm tracks, each chasing the one before it. Glancing back, I saw that Pierre had scooped his daughter up into his arms and was now stroking her hair, murmuring to her.

He held his little girl so tenderly, and I thought of Pappy, several towns away, wondering at his own daughter's whereabouts.

Stop crying, I told myself as I raked a hand across my face.

"Madge, she meant no harm," Keaton said beside me.

I held my hand up to silence him, shaking my head roughly.

Keaton fell quiet as we walked to the tree where Dame was tethered. Under it, Brom was sprawled out still asleep, his arms and legs agangle in the tall yellowing grass.

Blinking through the tears that clung to my lashes, I untied Dame's lead from the tree, then kicked at Brom's boot, saying, "Get up."

"Hmm?" Brom lifted an arm lazily to his face and rolled over.

"Get up!" I kicked him harder, now in his shin.

"Ow!" he hollered, sitting up. "Damn you, wench! Them shoes are pointy!"

I turned away from him and tried to hand Dame's lead over to Keaton.

He was staring at me, his blue eyes full of melancholy. I'd never seen him look so sad, and I was certain it wasn't because I'd kicked Brom.

I held out the lead to him, but he didn't take it. Dropping it to the ground, I started walking down the road toward Wexhall, longing to hear Brom damn me again.

***

Very little was said as we then walked for hours. Once we were settled for the night in a field outside of town, surrounded by other camping travelers, Brom wandered out beyond the trees, and I finally spoke.

"I don't know that I can well explain what happened to me earlier today," I said as we set out our bedrolls alongside the fire.

"Lulu's admiration of your birthmark startled you as you yourself abhor it so completely," Keaton said.

Stupidly, I stared at him, waiting for him to say more, wanting, hoping to understand myself as well as he seemed to.

He chuckled at my gaping mouth.

"Have you forgotten that I, too, look different than most, Madge? I see their flinches when people first behold me. It seems that when people do *not* recoil 'twould be the Balm of Gilead to the soul, but the unfamiliar brings its own discomforts and fears.

"The first time I looked deeply into Jane's eyes, I saw something there – neither pity nor scorn, both which I know so well. Nay, 'twas fondness – admiration even – and because of it, I could hardly speak to her."

A lump rose in my throat as I recalled how I'd fled from Yates in the woods.

"Stop looking into my heart, Keaton," I said with shaky laughter, sitting upon the log we'd pulled up to the fire ring.

"Ah, the heart!" he sighed and sat beside me. "Who can truly understand it?"

We were silent for a moment.

"What is she like, Keaton? This Rose of Thorneby?" I had wondered for so long.

Is she misshapen? Blind?

"Have I not told you of her?" Keaton began. "To merely speak of her will brighten the fire. First off, she is neither crooked nor tottering, if that thought was in your mind."

"Oh, nay I…I didn't suppose she was." I hoped my face did not betray me.

"Fret not, Madge. 'Tis a question I know all must have." There was no anger in his voice as he continued. "My Jane is good and kind, and bakes an excellent apple tart. I met her whilst singing at a wedding two years ago. She was standing guard over the tart table, as

176

all the wee boys would try to grab one and make off with it. One glance at her, waving a stick at any boy who came near, and I was smote to the heart. Truth be told, I forgot the words to the song I was then singing before all the guests!"

I laughed, trying unsuccessfully to imagine him faltering on stage.

"She looked up at me – as everyone there had – my mouth opening and closing like a fish, and she laughed. There was no spite in it, and I knew she wanted to talk with me afterwards, but as soon as I had recovered myself and finished my songs, I tucked my lute under my arm and hurried home. 'Twas a month before I determined I *would* speak to her if I ever saw her again, and then I had to wait *two* months before there was another wedding and I had the chance."

And she loves you, too, Keaton? I dared not ask.

Of course, she does! She's agreed to marry him. Dear Jane, you can see the genuine good in a person despite his appearance. You'd probably never break the heart of a little child.

Lulu's sobbing face had appeared in my mind again.

"Keaton, you understand me, yet when we left Vraimont, you looked so terribly sad at what had happened."

He sighed again, this time without happiness. "I saw Lulu lean in to kiss you and felt helpless to stop it though I suspected 'twould be your undoing. To her, your birthmark is good, the best of things, possibly."

"And then I dashed her love and joy against a stone," I murmured.

"'Twasn't on purpose," he said, reaching to pat my hand.

And she doesn't know how damning this mark has been in my own home. Though she and her father were pleased to look upon it, my own father cannot.

Ugh! Poor child. But what can I do for her now?

I took a deep breath and tried to push it all out of my mind.

"Think you I ought to apologize to the Man of Smells Aplenty?" I asked.

"What?" Keaton asked, his brow furrowed.

"Ought I apologize for kicking him?"

Keaton burst out, laughing with such force that it startled me.

"The *Man of Smells Aplenty!*"

He clapped his hand over his mouth as the log shook with our allied laughter. When he was finally able, Keaton dried his eyes, saying, "Such an apt name, I never heard! I would that *I* had thought of it!"

"What's funny?" Brom asked, lumbering back into camp.

"Ah, I'm sorry, Brom," Keaton replied, "but 'tis one of those things made unfunny in the retelling."

The juggler seemed content with this and, sitting, began to clean his nails with the knife he'd earlier used to cut our supper's onion.

How are we to keep things clean with him around? I wondered, then realized Keaton was addressing me again.

"In answer to your last question, Madge, no, I think not. Perhaps some good came of what you did."

In the firelight, I saw him wink and I knew that all was well between us. I could sleep that night lamenting how I'd hurt Lulu, but not fretting about the good minstrel in camp.

Gloves in Summer

This time, Brom's hands, encircling my waist, were gentle – surprising since he had cursed at me only a day earlier – and they seemed to linger even after he had set me against the pole.

Once again, I was in costume and had been carried across the stage to be propped up on its far end. Keaton had warned me that this would be the largest crowd we sang before. In spite of my fear, I tried to remain as rigid as a scarecrow would be.

Brom leaned forward to fuss with the back of my hat. With my face pressed to his shoulder, I felt the bulge of working muscles through his shirt, and my breath caught in my throat. Then he was gone, standing at centerstage as Farmer Brom, ready to be harassed by Crow Keaton.

That was strange, I thought, still feeling the pressure of his fingers on my waist. *And he didn't stink this time.*

With my head tipped just so, the flopping brim blocked all but the stage before me and the very front of the audience. This served my fluttery heart well that I wouldn't be put out of courage at the sight of the growing crowd. A few figures stood in my view, their faces rapt, amused by the mock feud that had begun to play out on the stage. Brom chased Keaton around a bit, but soon Keaton struck a chord on his lute and began to sing. Then came my cue to join in.

My voice started out wavering, but I kept my body still and sang on. Soon we were through the first song.

I did it!

As we started the second, an upright form stepped to the front of the crowd and stood watching us. Feminine in garb and shape, the hand this woman rested on the stage's edge was gloved, which seemed odd on such a warm day. This curiosity dulled the fright I felt at singing before the throng, and dimmed the image of Lulu's crumpled, wet face.

Such gloves!

They stretched from the tips of her fingers to beyond her elbows, disappearing under her sleeves.

Who would don such in this heat?

Tilting my head ever so slightly, I looked at where the woman's face should be and saw that it too was covered, even more so than my own. A veil was draped and precisely pinned in place on the brim of her hat, leaving only a narrow slit for her sight. Nary an inch of flesh, nor a lock of hair was to be seen.

I sang more easily as I watched the woman, hopeful that some movement would show a bit of her face or reveal something about her.

Nothing.

At the song's end, Keaton and Brom launched into another act at which the woman's shoulders occasionally shook with laughter. Brom began to juggle and then the third song was begun. Two more songs and some balancing of Keaton upon Brom's shoulders, and the woman did not stray from her spot at the stage's edge.

Why would she cover herself? By the looks of her clothing, she has money aplenty. I suppose even monied folk can be ugly old crones. But she doesn't move like an old woman. Perhaps she is bald*. But then why the gloves?*

"Good people of Wexhall!" Keaton called out, holding his lute out at his side. "If you deem our performance worthy, please prove such with a coin or two tossed into our juggler's hat."

At this, the woman clapped her gloved hands whilst a fair roar rose from beyond her. Startled, I lifted my head to observe the crowd which had swelled to the largest group of people I had ever seen assembled.

Good Lord! Look at all the people I sang to! I rejoiced at the sight, sinking down the length of the pole, happy to sit upon the solid, steady stage. *I was so curious about her, that I...*

Looking back to where the woman had been, I saw that she was gone.

"Pardon me," a shy voice said beside me. Startled, I turned to see a young boy, blond and blue-eyed, dressed in something like a uniform. He looked just a bit older than Lulu.

"Yes?"

"M'lady would speak with you and the little man also." He pointed to my right. "She will wait there for you."

Without staying for an answer, he ran off. Tilting my head back, I saw a carriage on the outskirts of the market square and beside it stood the boy, holding the gloved hand of a woman.

Oh!

It was her.

Perplexed, I rose and stepped across the stage to where Keaton was pirouetting clumsily, making a group of children laugh.

"Keat, a lady to see us." I motioned to the carriage.

Still playing the part, Keaton jigged across the stage and down its steps, overtaking me on the way. Brom still paced the stage, extending his hat to any late payers.

I hurried to keep up with Keaton's eager pace which ended in a deep bow to the woman.

"Keaton of Thorneby, Minstrel to All the World, at your service."

"Good day, Minstrel," said a voice, rich and soothing, unlike any I'd ever heard. "I've work for you and the scarecrow should you want it. Please step into my carriage that we may discuss it at length. I shall pay you for your time."

She stood upright and confident. Her clothes were indeed of a good quality, though neither fashionable nor showy. Still, with all her flesh covered, she left me with a slightly eerie feeling, though it was blunted by the way she was affectionately holding the boy's hand.

He is at ease with her.

"But of course," Keaton replied, heading to the open carriage door.

I followed, folding down the brim of my hat that it wouldn't be knocked off my head as I climbed the steps.

What could she want from us?

Stepping up into the vehicle behind Keaton and the woman, I drank in all the sights. Having ridden in only a wagon throughout my life, the grand carriage by comparison was a marvel. Two cloth-covered seats, much like settees, faced each other with very little leg room between. Small, curtained windows flanked the door. A nosegay of roses and lavender beautified the far wall of the compartment, filling the still air with a clean and pleasant odor.

There was nowhere to go other than beside Keaton who, as always, appeared at ease and amiable. My rump sank into the deeply cushioned seat.

Oh...this is the most comfortable place I've ever set my bottom!

The little boy followed us inside, swinging the door closed behind him before plopping down beside the woman who sat opposite us.

"Ugh, 'tis warm this day!" the woman sounded merry as she lifted off her hat.

Good god! I was thunderstruck.

Her skin was *brown*.

Not browned from working hours in the sun, nor brown from an abundant overlay of freckles, but truly and thoroughly brown as a chestnut.

I gaped as she placed her hat on her lap and proceeded to pull off her gloves.

Though the woman's skin was her most striking trait, her other features were a source of wonder as well. Her mouth, so round and pink, was like a rose blossoming above her chin.

Her face is abloom as mine is aflame, I marveled.

Her full lips parted, revealing rows of straight white teeth. Her nose was broad with flaring nostrils and the bits of hair peeping out of a cloth tied around her head were like puffs of black wool.

Such strange beauty, I've never imagined.

She gazed pleasantly back at us for a moment before extending her right hand to Keaton.

"I am called Lambie."

"I am very pleased to meet you, Lady Lambie," he said, reaching out to clutch the hand offered him.

Then she offered it to me.

'Tis as brown as her face, I thought, wondrously as I reached for it. *Well of course 'tis, simpleton!*

Keaton nudged me and murmured, "Oughtn't you doff your hat?"

"Oh, of course."

Letting go of Lambie, I fumbled with the wide-brimmed hat. As always when I revealed my face in anyone's presence, I didn't breathe the moment I knew my mark was seen and sat awkwardly staring down at the hat in my lap. After a brief silence, my eyes flitted to the little boy who regarded me for a moment, then glanced away and began kicking his feet as bored children are wont to do. Lifting my gaze higher, my eyes met Lambie's. There was at first mild surprise there followed by something akin to satisfaction.

"And your name, Scarecrow?" she asked softly.

"Madge." I bobbed my head.

"Madge *the Melodious*," Keaton corrected.

"Melodious? Aye, I heard that just moments ago. That suits my purposes beautifully," Lambie said, her rich voice filling the cavity of the carriage. "You see, I am of the household of a very dear elderly woman called Lady Fineness.

"Sadly, she is upon her deathbed. Nothing pleases her as does beautiful music and when I heard your songs, I knew I must bring you to her. I would be very pleased if your voices would soothe her during her last days. I know not what you earn whilst busking, but what I'm offering will far exceed it, I am sure. *And* you will be fed fine food and lodged in comfort for as long as you are with us.

"This is yours to keep regardless of your answer to my offer." She held out a gold coin to each of us. Pulling her gloves back on, she continued. "Willy and I will excuse ourselves that you may discuss this in privacy."

She donned her hat again and ducked out the door.

"Keaton!" I whispered fiercely, "in your travels have you ever seen…"

"No," he interrupted. "That is, I once saw two footmen of that color clinging to the back of a carriage, but never a grown woman who is clearly mistress to a grand estate. But Madge, your gawking was nearly profane."

This truth flustered me.

I, of all people, ought not be caught staring.

"What make you of her offer?" he asked, smoothing over his chastening. "I myself fancy reclining in luxury whilst strumming upon my lute…no hecklers hurling apple cores when chords are sour…sleeping in a real bed for a few nights. How could we say no?"

Oh, Keaton, nay! 'Twould keep us from Tersewell.

"Would we be safe in a strange household through the night?" I asked, floundering. "Who knows what might await us within those walls?"

"'Tis likely safer than sleeping out of doors with *no* walls!" Keaton laughed. Then he assumed a look of seriousness. "Or…is it that you fear *her*?"

"N-nay. That is, of course, she is strange to behold, but not in a fearsome manner. Oh! But what of Brom?"

Please, Keaton. I don't want to be stuck here in Wexhall. I must get home to Pappy.

"Ah, fret not. At times, Smells Aplenty's services are requested and *mine* are not. 'Tis the way of traveling performers, as he knows, and I shall treat him to a fine feast should this prove well for the two of us, which I do believe it shall."

"Think, Madge." He lifted the coin Lambie had granted him between his fingers. His eyes were bright. "If we serve the Lady Fineness thus, we may earn as much in a few days as if we traversed the entire countryside. I'm wary to sleep on such a pile of money each night, and if we went through Thorneby, I could leave it with my father for safekeeping. 'Tisn't far from here."

Thorneby is near? And Tersewell is just beyond it…

I bit my lip. Money held no draw for me, and though I was intrigued by Lambie, my only goal was to get to Tersewell and back to Trivington.

But I can't ruin this for him.

Unable to hold his gaze, I dropped my eyes, bit my lip and nodded slightly.

"Might I take that as agreement?" Keaton asked, nodding.

He will not be swayed, and I cannot continue without him. I owe him this goodness after breaking Lulu's heart right before his eyes.

As content as I could frame myself to be, I smiled and murmured, "Yes."

In an instant, Keaton pushed open the door and called out, "We've finished!"

Soon, Lambie and Willy were climbing back in. She, removing her hat again, smiled and asked, "Have you any questions, minstrels?"

"What of our juggler?" Keaton asked.

"I fear I've no use of him at this time." Lambie chuckled. "The Lady's eyesight is not good, and our ceilings are far too low for him to ply his trade by her bedside."

"Very well, Lady Lambie. Please excuse me for a moment to instruct him in the care of my mule, as we are pleased and grateful to accept your offer."

"Very good!" Lambie exclaimed as Keaton brushed past me and stepped out of the carriage.

We, two unusual women, regarded one another, and I watched as her smile broadened.

"I cover myself in the marketplace, for privacy when I desire such." Lambie motioned to the hat and gloves on her lap, then laughed, "...which is more often than not. The people of Wexhall are known to gape without pause."

She knows what it is to be different.

But soon, I will be like other girls. Ugh, I mustn't stay here long.

"Lady Lambie, it must be known that we cannot tarry here beyond three days. We're expected elsewhere and cannot disappoint those who await us."

I nearly flinched at the treason of my words.

Keaton needs to earn as much as possible that he might marry. Five days here could earn him a fortune!

But I must think of myself, as well. With his talent and determination, he will surely meet his goal. And my welfare is just as important, isn't it? Aye, Pappy is likely sick with worry.

"Very well, three days it shall be." Lambie answered, her voice and eyes softening. "I doubt the Lady Fineness will last even that long."

***

Not long after, I found myself inside the grandest of homes, following Lambie alongside Keaton up a flight of stairs. The bright red rug in the hallway was so thick that not a sound was made by any of our feet upon it.

"Please wait here a moment," Lambie said softly, when we had reached an ornately carved door. She entered the room and addressed someone inside. "How is she, Peggy?"

"Uneasy, I fear, Miss Lambie," a young voice replied.

"Go have some of Bessie's cake. I will stay, I and my guests. Please bid them come in as you go."

And what color is the skin of this 'Peggy', I wondered, watching the door silently swing open.

A girl came out and stood alongside the doorway, face down, to bob a curtsy. The hand with which she motioned us into the room was as pale as my own. Then she was gone, hurrying off down the hall.

It was dim beyond the door. Thick, gauzy curtains were draped over the two large windows, softening the midday sun as it shone in. And faint but unmistakable, there was the scent of illness, wafting through the air.

Elegant furniture lined the walls, all dwarfed by the large bed in the room's center. Four postered, it too was draped with curtains, these red with tassels, pulled back and tied with thick cords. It was the largest bed I had ever seen. Its covers were smoothly drawn across its surface, making it appear empty at first, but there, in the far-left corner, was a woman, frail and wizened. Her grey head was nearly swallowed by the fat pillow puffing up around it. Her arm, thin as kindling rested across her chest. The bulk of the rest of her body was lost under the heft of the bedclothes.

Motioning us toward two chairs at the end of the bed, Lambie knelt and began to smooth the woman's wispy hair back from her pale forehead.

"Good afternoon," she said, gently, though not quietly. "I've brought you something for your easement."

The ancient head turned slightly in our direction but it was clear the eyes were failing as the thin puckered lips below pursed themselves again and again.

"Please begin," Lambie said, nodding solemnly at us.

With Keaton's first gentle strum of the lute, I watched as the old woman's lips formed a sloppy smile of delight and her bony hand reached for Lambie's brown one.

"Ahh, yeth," she gasped as the soothing song continued.

Lambie giggled and said in the raised voice often reserved for the elderly, "I knew 'twould please you."

She leaned over to kiss the woman's forehead. The affection this action proved would have likely pleased me more had a raw memory of a kiss not resurfaced in that moment.

Ah, Lulu. I didn't mean to hurt you.

Keaton's voice joined his lute in song, the two sounds intertwining in the air all around us.

My mark is not used to being touched, let alone kissed...

At the song's end, the aged woman sighed, the smile still upon her face. "Thank you."

"'Tis all for you." Lambie said loudly, patting the wrinkled hand still in her grasp. Then she turned to me.

"Will you not join him, Madge?" she asked. "She is terribly fond of a good two-part. Oh, and Keaton, you needn't play only solemn songs. She's always loved lively tunes, and loudness cannot offend her faulty ears."

"Of course," Keaton replied and struck the first chord for 'Over the Golden Hills Anon'. The tempo picked up and he launched into the melody.

I beheld the two women, one upright and hale with firm skin as brown as a dark bay horse's coat, the other a shrunken wisp of white curled up on a pillow. Yet the affection flowing between them was one of the warmest displays I had ever seen.

And 'twill be one of the last between them, by the looks of her.

She's fond of a good two-part? God, help me to oblige.

My voice joined Keaton's readily as I watched the ancient head bob as well as it could to the raucous tune. After the final verse had ended, the ailing woman's eyes closed, though a smile remained on her face.

"I think you ought to rest now," Lambie said in a slightly quieter voice and moved as if to release her hand from the elderly woman's grip. "Oh, you want me to stay? Very well."

Lambie settled herself in a chair next to the bed, her hand still held fast.

"You may leave us now," she said to us, quieter yet. "You may make your way down to the parlor for some cake. In good time, the Lady will be awake to hear more. Thank you both. 'Twas lovely."

A sense of sanctity had fallen over the room and I merely bowed my head before walking out into the hallway, my mind more at peace than when I'd entered, Keaton at my side.

He gently squeezed my arm and whispered happily, "I heard you earlier upon the stage, and thought you did well, but just now, you sang, truly *sang* without reserve, Madge!"

I smiled and whispered back, "Yes, I suppose that I did."

"How was it so easy for you this time?"

Thinking for a moment as we padded down the hallway, I finally said, "Seeing the goodness in them and knowing that I could bring them joy made it easier."

"Good! Any time you are to sing, think on the gift you are giving to the people who will hear you." Keaton said, then swept his arms around to all the grandeur around us. "Oh ho! I would that Jane could see me now!"

He stopped at an open door and rubbed his hands together. "Ah! I believe we've found the parlor, and some of that Bessie's cake."

Whelks and Buckets

That evening, the frail old woman lay amongst her many covers, a tired but contented smile across her face as we sang several more songs to her.

For the first time in my life, I felt truly at ease, pleased even, singing in the presence of others. As Keaton had urged me to, I thought of the gift I was giving, and the music flowed out of me as naturally as breath itself.

Lambie sat nearby, surprising me by joining in occasionally. She possessed the same gift that Keaton had, able to hear the different parts of songs and enrich the music by giving them voice. The three of us together made a fine trio and the music we made helped me push the thoughts of weeping Lulu and frantic Pappy aside.

After we had finished 'On the Banks of the Clee', Lady Fineness lifted her hand as if calling for silence.

"Thank…you," she said laboriously, looking across the expanse of the bed though not seeming to really see us. Then, turning to Lambie, she said, "Sing one… of your… songs. They must…hear it."

I waited, curious.

The closest thing to a look of shyness flitted across Lambie's dark face as she glanced at us across the room. Then, clearing her throat, she opened her full lips and began to sing.

The song was low at first, merely a rumble from her mysterious depths, but it soon formed into words, clear yet strange. As the sound swelled into being, I closed my eyes and felt as if I was drifting away, called to unknown places by the thick, soothing sounds of a foreign tongue.

When the song ended, I sat for a moment longer in such heavy silence, my eyes still closed. The quiet was finally interrupted by a throaty chuckle from Lady Fineness.

"Mag...ical," she said. "Thank you...Granddaughter."

What?

My eyes flew open wide.

Lambie is her granddaughter*?*

I looked at Keaton who shook his head very slightly at me before asking, "Lady Lambie, whence comes such an enthralling tune?"

Taking a deep breath, Lambie clutched at the Lady Fineness's hand and replied, "'Tis a song of my mother."

"Who are your mother's people, Lady?" Keaton asked.

"She was born in a land very far away, an arid place, and was brought over the seas as a young woman." Lambie's eyes took on a plaintive look as she continued. "The cold of English winters was a shock to her every year though she survived it above ten times, and the clothing, she said, made her feel strangled each morning when she donned it.

"She yearned for the fruits of her homeland. Father brought her peaches and cherries, abricotts, anything sweet that grew. She would thank him and politely nibble on them, but even I, a young child, could see they were not what she longed for.

"She drew me many pictures of that which she missed the most from her homeland, but that was not her gifting, though I cherish each drawing still. Music was her talent. 'Twas her singing voice that won my father's heart when he met her in her homeland. He said this song ravished him when he first heard it." With that, she began another tune.

As Lambie's voice rose from a mere hum to a richness that filled the room, I tried to envision a village of people, all brown-skinned, wearing unusual clothes in a hot, dry land.

The world is full of vastly different people – uprooted French just miles from here and throngs of dark people across the seas.

Though I knew it was true, it felt a very foreign thought.

But where is a crowd of many red-marked folk such as myself?

Nowhere.

***

That night, Keaton and I sat alone at a large table where we dined on delicious pork roast and root vegetables. Peggy, the girl who had been sitting with Lady Fineness upon our arrival, lingered just inside the doorway, ready to tend to our needs. Though I wanted to ask Keaton what he thought of all we'd seen and heard that day in the Finenesses' household, I thought it rude to speak of it in Peggy's presence, and remained silent.

When we could eat and drink no more, she offered to lead us to our rooms for the night. Coming up the stairs behind her, I wondered about her. She looked to be thirteen years of age. Her figure had none of the grace typical in young girls, being shaped more like that of a burly boy, yet her voice was shy and sweet.

I had yet to see her face as she kept it ever toward the ground, even when speaking to us. This made her seem odd and though she was helpful, I felt uncomfortable in her company.

Perhaps that is why Babs was always telling me to look people in the eye.

After many turnings of corners in long hallways, she finally stopped at the open door of a dimly lit bedroom.

"Sir," she said, curtsying. Keaton bade us good night and disappeared inside.

Peggy and I ventured further down the hallway to another open door. Peering inside, I saw it was furnished better than even the best of the Gander's rooms. A few sticks of wood crackled in the fireplace and candles burned on the bedside table.

"Thank you," I said, stepping inside. Peggy surprised me by following me.

"Miss Lambie said you'd likely want a bath," she said, dragging a large wooden tub away from the wall. "Shall I fetch the water now?"

The thought of scrubbing all the grime of travel off of my body was certainly inviting, but the image of poor Peggy having to carry buckets and buckets of hot water up the stairs and down the halls made me pause. I knew well the drudgery of serving others, running to fetch whatever they fancied, and didn't want to lay that burden on another.

As I debated this, she was standing before me, her head down as ever.

"Don't worry, Miss," she murmured. "'Tisn't catching."

"Pardon me?" I asked, glancing around the room. "What isn't *catching*?"

"My face." She lifted it slightly but kept her eyes to the ground.

Oh.

Angry red spots covered her cheeks and chin, some crusted over with dried yellow pus.

My heart went out to her.

She thinks I cringe at the thought of her touch.

"Neither's mine," I said softly.

Her eyes flitted up to my face, grew wide, then dropped again to the floor.

There, now we have seen each other, two girls who hate to be looked upon.

"I only paused in answering your offer as that is a large tub and 'twould take many trips to fill it."

"'Tis no trouble, Miss," her voice brightened as her eyes met mine again. "I am strong, you see, and if I'm busy bringing water up to you, then someone else is washing the silver you used at supper."

Just as I prefer fetching mushrooms over gutting eels!

I laughed and she smiled timidly.

"Very well, Peggy," I said. "Fill that bath as full as you'd like."

Her smile grew and she went to the door, saying over her shoulder, "It won't take but a moment."

Soon she was looking over the steaming tub with pride, a bucket in her hand.

"I'll be back to empty it when I hear the bells toll ten o' the clock. There's a towel on the bed," she said, then motioned to a desk in the corner. "The soap and scrubber are there. You'll find other things for your comfort throughout the room. Use them freely."

Once she had gone, I stepped out of my dress and lowered myself into the water. Sinking in to my shoulders, I giggled, worrying it might overflow.

One trip too many, I fear, Peg.

I began to scrub myself clean with a cake of yellow soap that smelled like flowers. At first, the pleasant feeling of it delighted me, but then I started thinking.

Here you soak, served by some young girl whilst you ought be at the Gander serving its guests. And Pappy's probably so worried at your absence that he's not even able to tend to them himself.

Though the food in my stomach and the clean hot water lapping at my chin were proof of goodwill and kindness, I ached within and without.

I cannot stay here even three days, though I told Lambie I would.

Many coaches must pass through Wexhall. If I could just board one to Thorneby – Keaton said 'tisn't far from here -- then 'twould just be a matter of finding

Tersewell beyond it. Thence back to Trivington in another days' time or so.

Would Keaton feel abandoned? Nay, 'twas only four days past that I joined him and Brom. I've made no promises. They might even be relieved *at my parting. And I didn't start this journey to make friends and sing. I'm here to prove my faith and be healed that I can return home.*

In the meantime, I wish I could blunt Pappy's worry in some measure...

Oh!

I sat upright, sloshing water onto the floor. There, four feet from me upon the desk, was a quill pen, its white plume glowing faintly in the candlelight. Clambering out of the tub, I dried myself, and wrapped only in the towel, sat at the desk to delve into its drawers.

Paper...a bottle of ink...oh! Envelopes! Cut and folded envelopes! And a sealing stamp...

But ought I to use them?

Peggy said this room and its contents were for my comfort. What would bring more comfort than knowing Pappy was eased in his mind?

Drying my hands on the towel thoroughly, I smoothed a sheet of paper upon the desk and carefully uncorked the ink bottle. My caution was needless as, dipping the quill into its depths, I was dismayed to see it held nothing that might be spilled.

All these writing goods, but dry *ink?*

Pulling a lock of my damp hair together, I squeezed down the length of it, dripping a single drop of water into the bottle's belly. I scraped around inside with the quill, stirring whatever might be mixed as I thought about what to write. The rewetted ink was thin but visible upon the page as I began to write. With the dull nub, I formed these thick, untidy words:

I am well and shall soon return. ~ M

The sole sentence looked lonely on the vast expanse of paper, yet I knew the assurance it might bring and smiled as I folded the paper to slide it into an envelope. Tipping the candle, I spilt some wax upon the flap then pressed the sealing stamp into the molten puddle. Its image, a many-sailed ship with a large 'F' beneath it, cooled and hardened beneath my gaze. On the envelope's front I wrote:

Hazlett the Inn Keeper
The Gander's Wing
High Street ~ Trivington

Propping it up upon the desk, I stared at it a moment longer and murmured, "Thank You, for this provision."

I turned and saw the mess I'd made while bathing and determined to tidy it before the bells rang ten.

How many times have I wished Gander guests would make my cleaning jobs a bit easier?

When Peggy returned, I was sitting in the chair again, dressed in a white shift I'd found in the dresser drawer. She took away the water, one bucket at a time, smiling a little less shyly at me now. When she was nearly done, she asked, "Will there be anything else, Miss?"

"Yes, please," I said, my heart thumping. I held the letter out to her, wishing I could let her know how important it was to me. "Will you post this for me on the morrow?"

"Of course, Miss," she said as if it was the most natural thing in the world, holding it away from the damp front of her apron as she curtsied.

"Oh, and Peggy…"

She paused on her way to the door.

You are good, and kind and helpful, I wanted to say. *And that is true no matter how many red whelks mar your face.*

"You've a lovely smile," I said, instead. "It ought to be seen more."

Her smile grew as she reached for the knob. "Good night, Miss."

After snuffing out two of the three candles, I pulled back the top cover on the bed, to reveal the thinnest blanket I'd ever seen. It was of fine cloth and smooth. I knew what it was at once, something called a *bed sheet*. Pappy had spoken of them once after returning from London, wishing he could outfit the beds in the Gander's finer rooms with them.

"Only the finest," he'd said, then lamented. "But the finest I cannot always afford."

Slipping under the sheet, I felt its supple breadth cover me, dropping lightly against my tired body. It was a fineness indeed.

Pappy, I will return to you once my face is as fine as you want it to be.

I ran my fingers over the slippery bed sheet, far paler and smoother than the flesh of my own cheek. Thinking thus, I closed my eyes to hasten the passing of the night.

***

In the morning, I went downstairs where I joined Keaton at table.

"Good morrow, Madge!" he said happily, pulling the rind off of a strange looking fruit. "You must try one of these China Oranges before I eat them all. I confess this is my third!"

A silver dish held several more of the bright little orbs and I took one, setting it next to my plate that had already been piled with eggs and bacon.

As we finished, Lambie came into the breakfast room, staid and solemn. She seemed so different from the day before, barely murmuring a response as Keaton wished her a good morning.

What ails her?

The smooth skin of her dark hand was stark against the white tablecloth as she silently laid out six coins before us. With a small smile, she said, "Last night, the Lady Fineness slipped out of this world and into the next. Thank you for bringing joy to her final hours."

A tear slid down her face and splashed on the table as a little thrill of relief ran through me.

We may leave today! I thought and was immediately struck by guilt.

"Oh, Lady Lambie," Keaton said. "We are so sorry for your loss. 'Twas clear you loved her deeply."

Lambie bit her lower lip and nodded, then rubbed the fallen tear into the tablecloth as it was joined by another.

See what she meant to her? And here you rejoice at the woman's death!

I didn't poison *the woman! She died when she died.*

Lambie lifted her wet face to look at us.

"Your voices paired are a fine fit, but Madge…" she reached for my hand. "…when you sing, you oughtn't cover your face. I know well the vexation of prying eyes, but I heard you enshrouded on stage and then unveiled here, and there is no comparison. The beauty of your songs is heightened by your countenance."

I opened my mouth, flustered, then said nothing.

"Forgive me," she said, patting my hand. "Perhaps my grief has made me bold beyond what is proper, but I felt it so strongly I knew I must tell you. Please excuse me, as I have much business to attend to."

Keaton rose from the table and bowed his head. "Thank you, Lady Lambie."

I, too, stood and thanked her, trying not to show the joy I felt.

Twon't be long before I needn't cover my face at all, dear Lambie.

Dancing 'Round the Fire

Brom belched as he walked down the dusty road before us.

"That roast mutton was the finest I've had, maybe ever," he said.

"Glad you enjoyed it so," Keaton replied. "I said I'd treat you to a feast once we were done in Wexhall, and I am a man of my word."

"Thanks for that." Brom smiled, rubbing his belly. "Hey! Look!"

Down the road, off the side on a level spot, was parked a wagon.

Brom hurried off toward it.

"Who is it?" I asked, surprised at the vigor in his step.

"I believe 'tis Marvin and Mavis," Keaton replied, squinting in the distance. "We shall hear some fine fiddling before the night is done."

"Ugh," I muttered. "Doubtless only after sitting fireside all evening, hearing coarse talk between Mavis and Brom."

He laughed.

"Keaton," I said, watching as Brom reached the wagon and Marvin emerged from just beyond it. "I've wondered, how came you to know and travel with Brom?"

"Ah, we seem a mismatched pair, don't we? Well, we met last year on my maiden minstreling voyage across England. I was far from home having gotten all the way to Wexhall from Thorneby. Having slept rough and eaten poorly for a few days, I'd sung upon the stage there and was delighted to have made a bit of money. But as I descended the steps afterward, a man approached me. He wore a badge and looked lawful, so when he asked for the stage tax that I knew was due, I thought it only proper to hand over two pennies to him. He insisted upon a third though I was certain I'd been told aforehand by the stage-keeper 'twould be only two. I was sorry to see it go as every penny brought me closer to marrying Jane. Still, not wanting to gainsay him – and being sopping wet behind the ears at this new life I was hewing out for myself – I paid it over.

"Well, as soon as the coins hit his palm, a tall fellow in a scuffed leather jerkin stepped up behind him. 'Twas my first sight of Brom, and he looked fierce, a scowl on his face. The tax collector – not seeing him yet – smiled, thanked me and turned to go, nearly crashing into him.

" 'Give it back,' Brom growled. The strife I saw brewing confused me and at first, I supposed that Brom was robbing the tax collector! But in an instant, the third penny was being pressed back into my palm.

"*Oh, ho!* I thought. *This rough fellow stopped him from skimming a bit off the top for himself!* The smaller fellow turned again to go, but Brom's hand clamped down onto his shoulder. 'Give back *all* of it,' he said. Once coins one and two were back in my hand, Brom shoved the man off to the side, his face glowering, saying, 'I'll watch for you every time I come to Wexhall. Remember that.' The foiled rogue stumbled off into the crowd with only a quick glance back over his shoulder.

" 'And you,' Brom said to me. 'Don't jes' hand over money to anyone who pastes a sham badge on their chest. There're lots a people hangin' around stages, waitin' to pounce on us who climb down with a bit a money in our pockets. Now, go pay your tax where you ought and then you can use that third penny to buy me a tankard whilst I tell ya more things ya ought ta know.'

"Thus began my journey with the Man of Smells Aplenty!"

"Hmm," I said, marveling. "And to think *Brom* was the brains at first!"

Keaton snickered. "Yes. I know he's crass and seems to only chase his belly's yens, but there's a bit of wisdom in that head of his, and he's kind. Well, as *kind* as a brute is likely to be."

We were nearly to the wagon now.

"Keaton! Minstrel to All the World!" Marvin stood beside the road, his arms upraised in greeting. "And Madge!"

"Marvin!" Keaton called out.

"Hullo," I said, then moved to help Keaton release Dame from the cart as he and Marvin discussed their recent comings and goings.

I caught sight of Mavis, leaning against the wheel of the wagon, one of her sleeves slipping to reveal a smooth pale shoulder. She and Brom chatted, both of them looked delighted beyond what seemed reasonable.

On a stump, between two rocks, some playing cards lay face down, some fanned as if in play, others stacked in a pile.

We must have interrupted their game.

Stumbling into the campsite of others, I was uneasy at settling in. Once I had tethered Dame, I felt unneeded and wondered what to do. I stood stupidly for a moment beside the fire ring, then realized I could occupy myself for much time trying to light the fire.

Steeling myself, I stepped toward Brom and waited quietly until there was a break in their conversation. Finally, he glanced at me and I murmured, "Might I use your fire kit?"

"Ah, so you're a lighter of fires are you, Madge?" Mavis asked, her voice teasing.

'Look her in the eye,' I heard Babs say, and I did, as I said to her, "I've the will to try."

The somewhat smug look on her face dropped into one of surprise.

Ah, I was in costume when we first met and this is the first she's seen of my mark.

"Here," Brom said, pushing the kit into my hand, then chatted on to Mavis.

I walked to the fire ring where I knelt, striking the flint with the steel again and again until my knees and back began to ache. Many sparks flew, but nary a flame appeared to consume the little bit of char cloth. Still, my way was much improved from the first time I'd attempted to light a fire, and I thought I could accomplish it with a little more time.

Thank you, Thrin, for that.

I smiled at the thought of Thrin appearing before Mavis as she lounged against the wagon, saying, 'Thou ought to come to Meeting with me, friend.'

What would Mavis say in return?

"Yer goin' to wear me flint down to nothin'," Brom said beside me, then stooped down to take it from me. "Lemme do it."

Brom's history, as recently relayed to me, softened me to his gruffness and I didn't protest. Looking at his outstretched hand, I imagined it clamped down upon the would-be thief's shoulder, and I placed the flint and steel into it, moving aside.

Go on, Smells Aplenty. Flaunt your skills before her.

Mavis had come near the fire ring and sat down. Very soon, Brom had flames dancing before us at knee height.

Then, Mavis surprised me.

"Here, Madge. Sit by me." She motioned toward the other rock next to the stump with the playing cards upon it.

"I chose that one for me own ass," Brom protested, jovially.

"A *good* man would say nothing of it and just go get some firewood," Mavis responded playfully. "Come, Madge, tell me of yourself."

Brom lumbered off into the trees, his broad shoulders swaying, and I, shy again, stepped toward the place Mavis had offered.

Ugh. What am I to say?

Fortunately, I didn't need to answer this query as Mavis herself began to talk. As the three men milled around us, busy about camp, she prattled on and on. Her voice sounded different when she spoke to me rather than Brom. It was higher, sweeter and more lilting unlike the hushed throaty sounds she used with him. She told me of the places they'd been since we'd last seen them.

The earning had been good, she said, at *this* place but not at *that* place. The market, however, in *this* town afforded the best choice of ribbons and beads so she had been pleased to be there. She lifted her arm, jangling the many beaded bracelets she wore as she flipped back her hair from her face.

As was my custom with people, I didn't look often into her eyes as she spoke, but when I did, hers met mine. I could feel the draw of my mark on her eyes, though she most often resisted the urge to look directly upon it.

See it, Mavis, and be glad you have naught like it that you can flirt shamelessly with Brom.

I felt a bit guilty at my thoughts as she was being kind, though terribly dull.

"Hmm," she finally said, rising from her seat. "The sun will be gone soon and we ought to get supper together whilst there's light. Brommy, more firewood is needed."

'Brommy'? I smothered a smile and watched as Brom stood to do her bidding. *Oh, the power of a woman over a man with a yearning!*

"And Keaton, how is that Jane of yours?" Mavis asked. "As perfect as ever?"

I thought the question strange, almost mocking, but Keaton brightened as he threw more wood on the fire and said, "Yes, as a very few girls are."

He began to speak more of her, but Mavis cut in and was soon the only one talking again.

Everyone in camp had their tasks to bring about the meal and in due time we were all sitting around the fire in the gloaming, eating. Marvin and Mavis produced a potted brawn, and Keaton had evenly parceled out the bread and cooked cabbage we had bought before leaving Wexhall earlier that day.

As we ate, Mavis continued to talk, seemingly unaware that she was the only one doing so. Glancing around at the others, I wondered if it bothered them. Marvin sighed a couple of times, and Brom was no longer staring at her, but rather into the fire as he chewed and swallowed, then filled his mouth again.

Once the plates had been wiped down, there was a break in Mavis's jabber long enough for Marvin to say, "Thanks for that share of bread."

"Of course," Keaton replied. "Though surely you knew the cost of each mouthful you ate."

He wiggled his eyebrows merrily and began to bob a bit in his seat.

"Ha! You want to dance, do you, fine fellow?" Marvin said, rising from the log upon which he sat.

"Always and ever, dear fiddler!" Keaton jumped up as Marvin retrieved his instrument from the wagon.

"Very well, but first…" Marvin said as he produced a bottle seemingly from nowhere. "…a bit of Fiddler's Grease to loosen my arm."

He took a large swig then held it out to Brom. Brom drank then passed it to Keaton who smirked before tasting it.

"Mmm, subtle and refined," he said, wiping his lips and handing it to Mavis.

She gulped at it, silent at last.

"Here." She extended the bottle to me. "Have a sip of Granmammy's cordial."

Glancing at Keaton, I saw encouragement in his face, and lifted the bottle to my lips. As I tilted it back, a rush of something like liquid, something like vapor filled my mouth with fire. Nearly choking, I swallowed, spilling some down my bodice.

They all roared with laughter as I gasped and blinked, my nostrils burning.

"You duped me!" I sputtered, laughing. Shaking my slightly dizzy head, I capped the bottle and gave it back to Marvin.

He propped it against the log, a smile still on his face, steadied the fiddle under his chin and slowly drew the bow across the strings. A clear note cut through the evening air, teasing us with steadiness before it suddenly began to jump about. Soon my ears were full of the richest and liveliest of tunes that could be drawn from strings.

True to his word, Keaton began lurching about the campfire. Though it lacked beauty, his dance was one of the merriest sights I'd yet seen. Mavis began clapping in time and I joined her, laughing as the power of music surprised me once again.

Around the fire Keaton tromped wildly, leaping, then spinning until he was nearly toppled by a stick of firewood underfoot. At this, Mavis jumped up with the grace of a cat and grabbed onto his hands, crying out, "Careful, or we'll need to tie you up and toss you in the wagon!"

As someone who could prance and glide as easily as if she was simply breathing, Mavis led Keaton along in his joyful endeavor.

With Marvin's skill upon that fiddle and hers upon her feet, 'tis no wonder they can keep themselves fed by gracing the stage.

I watched, mesmerized as they circled the fire once again, my hands still clapping. Even Brom smiled as he gazed on them, his booted toes tapping the ground.

The sky continued to darken above us and with an abruptness that seemed rude, the song jarred to a halt, leaving the dancers breathless and laughing. The cordial was passed around for all to swig from – I declined this time – and Marvin began another tune, possibly more raucous than the first. One round into it, Keaton let go of Mavis and staggered over to me, extending his hand.

"Madge, you must dance!"

"I know not how," I protested.

"Clearly, neither do I!" Keaton assured me. "Let your body do what the music tells it!"

"But try to stay outta the fire!" Brom called as the sound from the fiddle swelled around us, his broad hands coming together with a formidable clap.

Lifted from my seat by the music itself, I was pulled around by Keaton and some mysterious force that seemed both outside of me and within me. If I was told to dance again the way I did that night without Marvin's fiddle to bewitch me, I wouldn't know how to try.

Keaton stumbled again, nearly taking me down with him. At this, Brom jumped up, hollering above the tune, "Go back to your nursemaid, Keat. I'll see to Madge."

Brom swooped in, his right-hand clasping onto my waist, his left grabbing my wrist, and began to propel me about. Keaton was back with Mavis. Brom pulled me past them as our shadows jumped along the ground around us. His abilities rivaled Mavis's, not in beauty but in power. Feeling possessed before, I now had to only hold onto him and lift my feet in time to the music. He did all the rest.

I suppose a juggler is likely to be an apt dancer, as good rhythm is needed for both.

When this song finally ended, my heaving chest could barely contain my pounding heart. I was so winded I couldn't even laugh. Brom held onto me still and I was glad for the support of his large hand on my waist as I felt light-headed.

Marvin laughed, the only one of us whose voice had not flown.

"Ah!" Keaton was finally able to bellow, clutching at his ribs. "My side is…stitched up…tight as…your bow, Marvin!"

He stumbled over to a seat and lowered himself to rest.

"Perhaps you will like this one," Marvin said, poising his bow before starting yet again.

"Nay!" Keaton protested, his mouth wide in a wheezing grin. "I can do no more!"

"Coward!" Marvin teased as he continued to play a slower song that flowed with the ease of a river.

As if needing no rest, Brom began to dance again, pulling me along.

We wheeled round, my shoes catching on little stones here and there, Brom steadying and carrying me in lulling circles. His hand slid from my side to my back, pulling me closer, pressing my shoulder and cheek against his chest. The heat from his body bore through his clothes, warming my already flushed face. I felt as if I was turning into water that surged with and around him. It was so strange.

And pleasant.

My face still pressed to his chest, I looked at the world spinning about me. The graceful rush of our shadows, the liveliness of the flames, the faces lit with joy and vigor, all melded together into something so pure and real.

And I was part of it, a large part of it.

Beaming, I tilted my head back and looked up into Brom's face. He looked different, but not because of the firelight. His face was entranced and he clutched me as if I was precious, relished even.

I felt beautiful.

When my mark is gone, I will feel like this every day.

My heart soared at the thought and something inside of me began to unknot itself. It was slow at first, but as it continued, I knew it was something that must stay firmly tied together. As the feeling grew, so did my urge to fight it.

Pushing against Brom's chest, I scrambled to free myself from his grip. It took a moment for him to release me and there was something in his eyes as he did so. It said he knew what was happening inside of me and he didn't want it to cease.

I gave him a hard shove and broke away entirely, hoping no one saw the look that passed between us. Forcing laughter, I stumbled to the fire ring proclaiming, "I need be done!"

My chest still heaving, I settled myself upon the rock and looked around at everyone. Keaton was laughing and swaying to the music. Marvin continued his playing, a solemn look of concentration possessing his face.

It looks as if I'm safe there.

But then, I looked at Mavis.

Still dancing alone, she glanced from me to Brom, then elegantly drifted to him, into his arms.

I grabbed a waterskin and drank swig after swig, unsure how else to busy myself. I didn't want to stare at them, circling and swaying in the firelight, but to slip into stark gravity might raise suspicion amongst the others as to what had happened to me.

What did *happen to me?*

I wasn't sure, but it pleased and terrified me in equal measure, just as knowing Yates had heard me sing so freely had done. This was different though. My insides quaked at remembrance of Brom's hand on my back and my face pressed against his warm, firm chest.

Am I aquiver at the thought of Brom? Ugh. How can that be?

"Y'alright, Madge?" Keaton asked, leaning in to take the waterskin from me.

"Yes, of course!" I said with a levity I could only hope for.

"You've drank it all!" he teased, tipping the spigot toward the ground, releasing only a few drops.

"Sorry." I blushed. "I've never flown about like that before. It made me thirsty!"

"No harm done." He chuckled. "Though I was hoping to wet my mouth before I lifted my lute. 'Tis customary to repay the fiddler, song for song."

Marvin finished the tune and soon, everyone was settled around the fire ring. I tried not to look at Brom, though I felt his eyes on me at times. I was thankful when Keaton began to play and sing as it was natural to stare into the fire as his voice floated up into the night sky.

"Don't you sing as well, Madge?" Marvin asked as the song came to an end.

Keaton cleared his throat keenly and threw me a knowing glance above the flames.

I smiled. "Yes…yes, I do."

"I should very much like to hear that," Marvin said, then gibed, "And remember, I gave you *three* songs."

"Very well then," I said, surprised I wasn't terribly nervous.

Lady Lambie is right. I oughtn't hide.

Keaton started another song, and this time I joined him. On the heels of my strange experience with Brom, I felt I was dreaming as our mingling voices rose into the air, dancing with the smoke. My throat relaxed further and my voice was pure and strong, then soft and gentle.

This is how I can sing.

I drifted along on the joy and beauty of the sound until our voices held out the final note together, fading it into the silence of the darkness.

"Beautiful," Marvin said quietly when the final strain had died.

"Ha ha!" Keaton laughed, pushing his lute aside to clap me on the shoulder. "I'd venture to say that was your best yet, Madge! Well done!"

My face warmed at his praise.

See, Mavis? You can dance and flirt and tease, but I, too, have my gifts.

Though not intending to, my eyes flitted toward her face. I thought, foolishly perhaps, that she who had earlier offered me a seat by the fire and chatted happily to me for hours, would be pleased to see that I was more than just a large red blotch.

But her face was churlish as her eyes slid from me to Brom.

I peeked at him, and noted his eyes were already resting on my face. In the days since I'd met and traveled with him, Brom had never truly looked at me. At least, not that I'd seen, not in a silent, assessing manner.

So much can be said with one glimpse. Words cannot capture and convey what eyes can. He admired me, and – even though my beholder was a crass, overgrown boy – my heart swelled.

In that moment, I again felt beautiful.

'I soon found that I felt the happiest when I sang,' Keaton had told me days earlier. *'I grew keen to live in that moment as oft as possible.'*

I understand now, Keaton.

Turning to the minstrel at my side, I cleared my throat and said. "Let's sing 'Beneath the Verdant Boughs'."

The Queen's Face

The sound of squealing startled me from my slumber.
But what I saw when I opened my eyes was even more
jarring. Mavis's face was just inches above my own.

"I told you!" she screeched as she crouched over me.

What...!

"I don't see it," Marvin said, squinting beside her.

Gasping, I covered my face with my hands and sat up.
Mavis hovered so closely that my head nearly knocked
into hers.

"Put your hands down," she said, tugging on my wrist.
"I'm trying to show them something."

I pulled my arm free from her and noticed a small piece
of paper in her other hand. She held it beside my face.

"Madge looks *just* like her," she insisted, looking at it,
then back at me. "Don't you think so, Brom?"

"Dunno," he muttered, groggily from under his blanket,
a few feet away.

"I *am* right! Madge shall see for herself," she said
smugly. Letting go of my arm, she hurried off to the
wagon.

My head ached with the abrupt awakening. The sky was well lit though there was yet the chill of early morning in the air. I shivered and wrapped my blanket around me tighter, relieved Mavis no longer loomed near me.

But then she was back, crouching at my bedside, this time shoving at me a small looking glass, about the size of a small plate. She held it by its long handle, its shiny surface a finger's length from my nose. In its depths, I caught sight of my tangled hair and the little crumbles of sleep in my eyes. Of course, there was also my spot, as large and red as ever, glaring back at me.

"See?" Mavis said, putting the paper – I saw now it was a playing card bearing the image of a woman– alongside the mirror. "An exact likeness! She's even got a mark on her cheek, though not *nearly* as big as yours."

She tilted the glass slightly and it caught the rays of the rising sun behind me, channeling their brilliance into my eyes.

"Ugh!" Blinded, I thrust my arms out wildly. "Stop it!

"Careful!" she shrieked as the looking glass fell onto my lap. She picked it up and hugged it to her belly. "This cost a lot of money. You could have *broken* it."

"Leave me alone," I hissed. It exited my mouth naturally, but the bitter feel of it on my tongue was foreign.

I never speak like that to anyone. I don't like who I am when I'm near you, Mavis.

Taking a deep breath, I determined to behave more like my wonted self and calmly pushed my blanket away to stand up, saying nothing more.

"You needn't be so cross," she continued, pursing her lips. The way she knelt on the ground was odd, her bosom thrust over the top of the mirror she still cradled. She tilted her head dramatically as her eyes slid over towards Brom.

He was sitting up now, his hair sticking up wildly, an amused grin on his stubbly face.

It's all a show! Play-acting for Brom!

He chuckled. "Shoulda known 'twouldn't be long afore the wenches went to war."

Marvin, stirring the ashes from the previous night's fire, hmphed his agreement.

"I was only trying to show everyone how much Madge looks like the Queen of Spades," Mavis pouted.

I'll have none of this, none of you, Mavis, I determined, smoothing my skirt over my legs, then patting my hair into place.

Where is my ally?

Looking around the site, I tried to remain calm though I saw Keaton nowhere. His blankets were folded neatly and set upon a rock.

231

Fret not. I peered out into the woods. *Everyone is allowed a trip out into the woods. He will return.*

Brom stood and stumbled off into the trees beyond while I folded my own blanket.

Mavis said nothing more as she lifted the mirror before her own face and began to primp.

A twig snapped behind me, and to my relief, Keaton ambled back into the campsite.

"Good morning," he said, cheerfully.

Mavis murmured a reply while Marvin shoved a few things into a sack.

Catching sight of my face, Keaton asked, "Y'alright, Madge?"

Ugh. I won't *continue what Mavis has started.*

"Yes," I said, yawning, then stretching. "Just slept a bit askew. My back is cricked."

"Ah. Nothing walking a few furlongs won't cure," he said, brightly.

"You're quite merry this morning." I forced a smile. "Oh! Of course. We draw ever nearer to Thorneby."

At this, he wiggled his eyebrows.

"Nay, don't go that way!" Mavis cut in, then slinked up to him to lay her head on his shoulder. "I hoped we'd all travel together for a spell."

My stomach lurched and I feigned amusement "I assure you, Mavis, *nothing* will sway Keaton from getting to Thorneby as soon as he can."

"But all the prudeys are around there, scaring people off," she insisted. "'Tisn't good for making money."

"Mavis is right, Keaton," Marvin said, brushing his horse's flank. "They've cinched up things in the market places 'round there. Last time we went through, they wouldn't let us have the stage at all. I even offered twice the stage tax, but the keeper said no as he didn't want any trouble from zealots."

"I'm well aware," Keaton replied. "I skirted some of that even in Trivington but I suspect 'tis worse for you lot than for us. We all know what passions fiddling and dancing can stir up within the common folk!"

My face flushed, remembering the strange occurrence from the evening before.

"But I'll choose carefully what songs we play," Keaton continued. "None of the bawdier ones. I'm off to see Jane, and nothing will waylay me!"

"Hmm," Mavis said. "Well perhaps we can borrow Brom and rejoin you back in Wexhall next week."

"Ask him. He's his own man," Keaton replied, putting his blankets into the cart.

I headed out into the woods myself for a few moments.

Rejoin Mavis in Wexhall? The thought would have plunged me into gloom had I not trusted that by the next week, I would be healed and home.

Tersewell, I thought, staring up at the vast and gnarled oak branches above my head. The sky was bright and blue beyond them. *I shall see you very soon.*

After taking a moment to breath in the chilly morning air, I was ready to return to the others. Knowing we would be parting ways with the siblings, I felt as eager to get going as Keaton seemed, and within a few moments, we were packed up to tread down the road. We all walked together at first, but at the nearest fork, we halted to say our goodbyes.

Brom chose to turn to the right with Keaton and me, though Mavis hung on him and scowled prettily, her eyebrows coming together over her dark eyes.

Marvin bowed to us from his wagon seat, pulling on his beard. Once Mavis had clambered up to sit beside him, she tipped her head, saying in a sing-song voice, "The pleasure was all mine. I hope we'll all meet again soon."

With the air of a princess, she reached her hand down toward me. "Goodbye, Madge."

"Hmm, and to you," I murmured, pinching the tips of her fingers and determining I would never touch her hand again once I had released it.

With a few creaks and the dusty plodding of their horse, Marvin and Mavis started off down the road to the left.

A Few Coins More

By noon, we had stopped to eat our dinner near a small stream.

"If I remember aright," Keaton said, chewing his bread and pointing east. "There is a small town just beyond that hill. Though we weren't there for the morning market, there may be a crowd for us this afternoon."

"Not likely," Brom answered, loosening the ties on his jerkin.

"Perhaps not," Keaton conceded. "Nevertheless, I'll take every chance I can to earn a little money more. What are you doing, Brom?"

Brom pulled his jerkin and then his shirt over his head. "Thought I'd wash as the stream's here."

"Oh, well please don't be long about it as I'd like to get going." Keaton laid back on the grass and closed his eyes.

Brom grunted as he stepped toward the water, and into the sunlight.

I watched as his broad back, shining white, moved away from me. The quick glimpse I'd had of his chest, revealed an even thatch of short chestnut-colored hair across its breadth.

He knelt by the water, scooping some up to splash under his arms and over his face. Again, and again, he dipped his hands to pour water over his body, his arms and shoulders looking so very unlike the other bare limbs I'd seen in my life – delightfully so. I thought of Babs's arms with her sleeves pushed up above her elbows, deftly kneading bread dough.

Yes, men and women are different, indeed.

Suddenly, he turned his head and I dropped my gaze, mortified that he might have seen me watching him.

"Keaton," I hurried to quietly say, "I've been wanting to tell you…I'd like to give you some money."

"What?" He opened his eyes and lifted his head from the ground, puzzled.

"I am so grateful for the guidance and kindness you've shown me, and I'd be happy to know it helped you and Jane to marry." It wasn't a speech I'd planned, but as it exited my mouth, it pleased me, its truth undeniable.

However, he looked disapproving as he sat up and said, "I couldn't take what you've earned."

"I'd have earned *nothing* if 'twasn't for you," I insisted.

Brom stood up by the streamside, looking as if he would make his way back toward us.

"Nay," Keaton said. "Your offer is kind, but think, Madge, I'd be a fool to rely on it. If I cannot earn what I need on my own, I've no business taking a wife. You won't *always* be with us. And what of next year when my first baby's on the way?"

He smiled, clearly pleased at the thought, then reached to grab my hand.

"And you, Madge. I've been thinking." He grew serious again. "After our stay in Thorneby, would you like to...that is, would you be *ready* to go back to Trivington?

"I'd miss you as you've become a bolder singer than I ever thought possible – you sounded angelic last night! But could you face your father, you think?" He squeezed my hand and gazed at me thoughtfully.

"Oh, umm..." I stammered.

Ought I tell him of Tersewell?

Suddenly, Brom tromped back toward us, dripping from head to waist.

"Yes, Keaton," I answered in a rush. "I think I'll be ready."

"Excellent," he said, smiling warmly as he let go of my hand. "You've a nice little bit of money now..."

Oh Keaton, with all of your uncanny wisdom, 'tis a wonder you still think that money *is what I need!*

Standing three feet away, Brom shook his wet head like a dog, spattering us both with countless chilly drops.

"Hey!" Keaton laughed and stood up from the ground, turning to untether Dame. "I bathed just three days past!"

My eyes were looking anywhere but at Brom as I began to push myself up off the ground. His large hand dropped into view, outstretched to haul me up. Uncomfortably, I grasped it, noting how cool it was after many dippings into the stream. He pulled much harder than he needed to and, standing, I found my face just inches from his bare chest.

I murmured my thanks and stepped away quickly, ashamed of how fluttery my heart felt.

It's Brom, I reminded myself. *Vile, beastly Brom!*

***

Our busking that day was not very profitable, just enough to cover the cost of our evening meal. Fortunately, there had been no stage there, and therefore no stage tax was required of us.

Bolstered by my singing success the night before, I felt less fearful as I stood, bare-headed, before all who stopped to listen. Still, I let my hair hang forward and kept my eyes to the ground as I sang out.

Brom juggled between songs, first with four balls, then adding one each time till he was up to six. Before we sang our final song, he juggled beanbags. I suspected he saved those for last because he could manage eight at a time and toss them quite high. Just as he finished, I heard a woman in the crowd ask the man standing beside her, "He's not quite Romney, is he?"

In reply, the man smirked and shook his head as they walked away.

I thought I saw Brom's back stiffen but forgot about it as Keaton and I began our final song.

***

That evening, just as Keaton and I were setting up camp, Brom walked to a nearby clearing with his hands full of beanbags. Soon, they were flying up into the air, but strangely, within seconds they would all drop. I stopped brushing out Dame's coat to watch for a long moment.

"What's he doing?" I asked Keaton, quietly.

"Hm?" He stopped fiddling with the spit frame to look. "He's practicing, poor fellow."

"What mean you?" I asked.

His voice dropped a bit lower. "Truth be told, Madge, as far as jugglers go, Brom's not too highly regarded. He can, of course, out-juggle you or me, but if he was to be lined up with others of his trade, he'd not fare well."

Romney.

"Who's Romney?" I whispered.

"Did someone mention him today?" Keaton lifted his eyebrows to which I nodded.

"See *Romney* juggle once and you'll know his name forever and always," Keaton said. "He juggles eight balls at a time with ease, *and* he tumbles. Even tumbles *whilst* juggling! He's a small wiry fellow, quick and bendy as can be. Can you imagine Brom turning a somersault?"

I couldn't laugh at the ridiculous notion.

"So, now and then, Brom tries to add more to his act, though he's not gained much from what I see. Perhaps I shouldn't admit this, but it's been my boon that his skills are lacking, as he mightn't travel with me if he could woo the crowds without my songs to balance it out. I've told you, we both benefit from our mismatched arrangement."

I watched Brom for another moment, silently willing the bags to stay aloft, but they fell with regularity as I saw he was launching not the usual eight, but ten.

Poor fellow, indeed.

He paused, looking as if he may have finished. Determined not to be caught watching him twice in one day, I turned and searched for something to do. Grabbing my pack, I dumped it out onto my blanket, seeking my comb. Out fluttered a small piece of paper which fell to rest, face up, with my other things. I gasped.

It was the Queen of Spades.

When did she put that in there?

The thought of Mavis rifling through my things made my skin itch, made me want to look at every item, deciding what to rid myself of simply because she may have touched it.

Don't be ridiculous. I have so little with me. There is naught to spare.

Why would she do this? How foolish to spoil an entire deck of cards just for spite!

Noting my own surpassing wisdom was little comfort.

Picking the card up, I stared at it. Through the years, I had seen many playing cards in the Gander's dining room. Some had been crisp and colorful, others tattered and plain. This simple card was black and white, printed on thin paper. The queen was thick around her middle, decked in a stiff looking dress and wide head cloth. In her hands, she held a spade against her chest as if it was a cherished flower. Her eyes were too large for her small face and her nose was a sharp beak, jutting out above her prim little mouth. There, on her left cheek was a spot, just as Mavis had said, but it was small and black, likely a blob of ink that fell awry as the card was printed. If anything, it looked like a beauty patch, not a birthmark.

Why is Mavis so unkind?

"What's that?" Keaton asked.

"Nothing," I muttered, trying to keep the card from quivering in my hand.

"Your eyes are burning a hole right through it," Keaton said, drawing near to me. "What is it?"

I sighed and shook my head. "Mavis was insisting this morning that I look exactly like the Queen of Spades. She must have hidden this in my bag."

He turned my hand toward him that he might see for himself.

"What?" he scoffed. "I see no likeness."

"Nor do I. Why does she hate me so?"

"'Tisn't hate, dear one," he took the card from me and tore it in half.

"What mean you?"

"Isn't it clear?" Keaton asked, surprise in his eyes. "She's jealous of you!"

"*Jealous*?" I laughed harshly. "Don't be daft!"

From the corner of my eye, I saw Brom coming toward us, his hands full of beanbags.

"Of course, she is! I saw it when we were singing last night. Ah! You've never heard her *sing*, have you? Well, she dances very well, but her singing is merely middling though she does it every chance she gets or did at least when I last met with her."

Jealous? Could it be true?

"But she was sweet as a kitten to me when we first arrived last night…offered me a seat and…and…"

"Yes! That was *before* she heard you sing!"

And before she saw me dancing with Brom. It started to make sense though it was hard to believe. I understood what he was saying but accepting it as truth felt so very queer.

If I was able to step back and watch two other *girls in this matter, I might believe it.*

"But she's pretty…" I said, then stopped, silent in disbelief.

Brom was beside us now.

"Mavis? Yer prettier than her," he said.

I felt as if I'd been hit upside the head.

"Least y'are when yer smilin' and not shrinkin' away from everyone an' everythin'," he added.

Prettier than Mavis? He finds me pretty at all*?*

"But, but…my mark."

"Mark?" asked Brom.

I knew not whether he was in earnest or in jest, if *all* he was saying was for his own boorish amusement.

"The big, red blotch on my face, Brom!" I snapped, pointing at it.

"That?" He furrowed his brow. "I saw it at the first, but hardly think of it now."

What? How could anyone *look at me without this monstrous flame jumping out at them?* I nearly sputtered.

But his face was still and as thoughtful as I'd ever seen it.

Is he pitying me?

Silently, I considered this, then calmly said, "Lies bring little comfort, Brom, no matter how kind."

"Ugh. Never mind," he muttered. "Why even bother talkin' to wenches? Here, gimme that paper to start the fire."

He took the two card halves from Keaton and stalked off to a clear space, pulling out his fire kit.

"We speak truth, Madge," Keaton said quietly, then walked the spit frame over to Brom.

Do they? I wondered. *Keaton would likely lie to heal my heart, but Brom? He knows nothing of guile, saying whatever comes into his mind. Whether it be proper or not, wise or not, he simply speaks.*

And he says I'm pretty.

***

Later that night, I was standing in a stream, singing, hiking my skirt up above my knees to keep it out of the water. When I saw Yates approaching me, I paused my song.

"I shan't run from you this time," I laughed.

He splashed into the flow, his eyes fixed on mine. As he drew nearer, I dropped my gaze to the sparkling water below, and watched as his feet came to stand toe to toe with mine.

"I've made this for you," he said, holding out to me a single shoe.

I took it, examining the sides, covered in intricate, colorful embroidery. Shy to look up at him again, I murmured, "Thank you."

"Madge," I heard and when I lifted my face, it was Brom standing before me, bare chested, his eyes peering as steadily into mine as Yates's had a moment earlier.

He plucked the shoe out of my hand and dropped it in the water. I opened my mouth to protest, but he was reaching toward me again, this time to push my hair back from my face.

The shoe floated further downstream and I reached to grab it, but his arm was around me, grasping at the small of my back.

I woke with my hands clutching at the air above me, my heart pounding furiously.

Frantically groping under the blanket, I felt the reassuring lumps of both shoes against my hip. I'd slept every night since leaving home with them tucked against my side thus. Smoothing my blankets over me, I breathed slowly and deeply, waiting for my heart to resume its normal pace.

How stupid. Half-naked Brom stealing *my shoe!*

I snickered at the thought, hearing the offender snoring lightly, several feet away.

But it seemed so real. I could feel the cool water flowing around my ankles. And his hand pressing against my back.

Ugh! It's Brom*!*

Are these the evil thoughts that zealots call 'carnal' and warn against. They come, unbidden. I cannot stay awake just to keep them at bay!

Nay, but you have strayed in your purpose. 'Twas just a few days ago that the Inward Light told you to seek healing at Tersewell.

That is not exactly what was said...

Lyle the Toothless said 'tis impossible to please God without faith, and just after, the smithy spoke of Christ healing the blind man at the pool. Have you forgotten already?

So much has happened in the days since! Little Lulu kissed my mark, I met Lambie, I've sung beautifully without shame...I learned another girl is actually envious of me...I've quaked at the touch of Sir Smells Aplenty's hand!

Do you still want healing?

The strife of my two minds raged on. Babs had badgered me for years, both in the kitchen and in my thoughts, but never so heartlessly as this. And not even Thrin – in the two days I knew her – who readily voiced her thoughts as if they were proven truths, harangued me as I did myself now.

Do you no longer care if Pappy can look upon you or not?

That is all *I care about!*

Truly? When did you last pray? And you've yet to tell Keaton of what awaits you at Tersewell. He still thinks you want to earn money!

But I don't know that he would understand.

If you had true *faith then you'd care not what he thought, nor if he understood. You must prove your faith. If it's lacking then God will be displeased and Pappy will never see you without shame again.*

Pressing my hand to my aching head, I made a vow.

Henceforth, I will stay the course. When I must sing, I will, but I will not let the praise of others – or Brom's attention – beguile me. Scripture promises that if my faith is pure, then God will be pleased with me. I will seek out Tersewell and not let anything keep me from it.

Determining such quieted my mind somewhat, though little flares of protest on either side would spark up to rile me. It was a full hour, certainly, before I was able to fall back asleep.

A Glimpse of Arches

The sky was just lightening, when I awoke. Keaton was up, bustling around camp, making more noise than usual. Brom slept on, his head lolling upon the bare ground, his mouth agape. We pretended to throw bits of bread into it as we ate our breakfast and I was pleased to laugh with my friend after having slept poorly the night before.

Tell him of Tersewell.

Later. I'm savoring this time with him as I'll be gone soon.

Seeing that the battle of my two selves threatened to begin again, I stooped down and grabbed onto Brom to shake him awake. His shoulder felt firm and powerful in my grip, reminding me of his manly form as he bathed the day before.

Stop it! Ugh. This day is not *beginning well.*

After he stumbled around camp, securing his things together, we set out.

Soon, Keaton began commenting on how the land around us was getting more and more familiar, a spring in his tottering step.

"Come along, Dame," he'd say, patting her rump. "Look lively."

Throughout the morning, I asked both Brom and Keaton more questions than I had in all the days we'd been together. I queried the names of their siblings, what were their first memories, which foods most delighted them – anything to keep from being alone with my thoughts.

I must seem like Mavis, blabbing on endlessly, though I'm asking about them, whereas she spoke only of herself.

As morning neared noon, I noticed in the distance a huge, jagged wall, vaulting up into the sky. Blindingly white in the sunlight, it had at least five arched windows, the rest of it disappearing into the trees.

"What's that place, Keaton?" I asked. Though it appeared to be crumbling from the top down, it was beautiful.

"Hmm?" He looked toward the wall. "Oh, 'tis an old abbey called Tersewell."

My heart jumped into my throat.

This is Tersewell? But I thought 'twas past Thorneby.

"Actually, you may recall," he continued, "that Lottie spoke of it on the day we first met."

"Oh...aye, I *do* remember," I feigned minor recollection. "She mentioned it a few times even before her mind left her."

God, You've led me right *to it!*

The thick woods abutting the road allowed no glimpse of any buildings besides the one wall.

But where are the waters? In the woods? Near the arched wall?

Ahead, I saw a rutted drive that snaked out of the abbey's woods to join the road we traveled. As I considered how I might find the well, a horse-drawn wagon appeared, coming down the drive. A man, a farmer by the look of him, drove it whilst a younger fellow rode beside him. He turned toward us on the road and we were soon within earshot of each other.

Keaton tipped his hat, calling out, "Greetings, good men!"

The farmer nodded. His clothes were dusty and he looked uneasy, but he stopped the wagon.

"If *I* don't take it, some'un else will and my walls need shorin' up same as any'uns," he said as if we'd already been in conversation.

What confession is this?

"Pardon me?" Keaton said as Brom and I exchanged glances.

"Pa, they don't know what yer speakin' of," the young man muttered, looking bored and annoyed.

"The stone, of course," the farmer said, tipping his head at the wagon bed. It was loaded with large pale blocks of hewn stone. "I don't feel quite right takin' it, but the Roundheads like to see it go."

"How many times've I gotta tell ya, Pa? They ain't *Roundheads*," the young man scoffed. "Haven't been for years."

The farmer turned to him and hissed, "Well they're just like those we called Roundheads in *my* day – threatenin' and fightin' any'un that gainsays 'em – destroyin' anythin' that affronts 'em."

The rebuked son rolled his eyes as the farmer warily looked down the road in either direction and turned back to us, his gaze lingering on Keaton.

"You've a look of pilgrims about you," he nearly whispered. "If that's yer business, I suggest you go 'bout it most carefully. Not long ago, them Roundies filled the well with sand to stave off them who come for healin'."

Come for healing?

My heart began to pound fiercely.

His son made a sound of disgust and shook his head. "Ugh, Pa…"

254

"Thank you for fair warning, sir," Keaton said in serious tones, "but I assure you we're just two minstrels and a juggler on our way to Thorneby."

"Hmph!" the farmer gibed. "Minstrels and jugglers? Them Roundies don't like *you* lot, either! But I've said my piece. Good day to ya."

With a slap of the reins, he started the horses off at a slow pull.

"And to you, sir," Keaton responded.

The son threw us all a look of embarrassed apology as the wagon rolled forward.

"What was he blatherin' about'?" Brom asked, not as quietly as he ought.

"You understood it as well as I," Keaton murmured, chuckling as he stepped onward.

"But 'healing', what meant he by that?" I asked with as amused a tone as I could muster.

"'Tis said the waters of Tersewell cure those who seek them out."

"Healin' of what sort?" Brom asked, looking down at his arms, flexing them. "Would they make me stronger?"

I stared at my pacing feet, trying not to appear eager for Keaton's answer, thankful that Brom was asking questions, no matter how silly they might be.

Keaton laughed. "I've heard tales of stomach problems cured…skin ailments – oh! – and barrenness! Did you want some fruit in that womb of yours, Brom?"

Skin ailments.

We drew closer to the drive that could take me up toward the well.

Now. Tell him now – even with Brom here – that you have come for healing.

But…

"Where are you going?" Keaton's question interrupted my fretful parley.

I looked up to see that Brom was hurrying ahead.

"I want to see this place," he called over his shoulder as he stepped onto the drive, then gruffly added, "You stay here and lookout for *Roundies*."

"You'd leave us to be skewered, would you?" Keaton hollered, laughing as he turned to me. "The ruins *are* quite lovely and 'tis nearly time for dinner. We might as well rest here a bit."

"Aye. Then I can tell Babs of it when I'm back home."

'Tis a cowardly reply. Tell him your entire journey was for nothing but this.

But why, when he can just watch *the healing itself?*

With my head abuzz, we veered up the drive after Brom. Coming around a bend in the lane, we emerged from the wood and the ruins rose up before us. The framework of a few buildings stuck out of the ground like broken bones on a platter, picked clean of meat. Most impressive of all was the wall with its arched windows, soaring straight up into the blue sky. There was still a seeming order to the place though it was overgrown with tall grasses and brambles, and loose piles of rock, like what had filled the farmer's wagon, were scattered across the grounds. Continuing on, the lane took us through a graveyard, its many tilted headstones rough with age, some green with moss.

Brom was at the wall's base, running his hand over it as he walked its length. He glanced back at us, the bottoms of the windows high above his head.

Go find the well.

Instead, I went to the wall itself and pretended to examine the grooves and fanciful curves that had been chiseled into its surface.

"Bread and brawn!" Keaton called out, pulling the food from a sack and settling himself in the shade of the wall.

This brought Brom back from his delving and I joined them, though slowly. The men made a quick meal of it, neither seeming to notice how little I ate.

"Ugh. My feet are aching," Keaton muttered, closing his eyes as he leaned back against the wall. "How often

I wish Dame was strong enough to carry me *and* pull the cart."

Standing, Brom took a drink of water, then asked, "Where's this magic well?"

Keaton waved. "Just beyond the arches, under a large oak tree."

Dropping the waterskin, Brom strode off. With my heart in my mouth, I followed him and came around the edge of the wall to see the tree Keaton had mentioned. Underneath it, a group of flat stones were embedded in the ground. Brom stood beside them, staring down.

"That farmer's not barmy after all. *'Tis* full of sand," he said, then knelt.

I felt light-headed as I made my way toward him.

Is this when I shall be healed, God? 'Tis not how nor when I expected.

The ground was spongy, sucking at my shoes with each step I took. Drawing near, I saw the stones were laid in the form of a star and in its center was a pit of wet sand with less than an inch of water at its surface. My heart sank at the sight.

'Tis spoiled.

Where is your faith? The waters are still here.

I suppose, but what am I to do with them?

"No magic here," Brom muttered, standing then striding off back towards the wall.

I cannot drink them as they're not deep enough to dip my hand. Ought I to plaster my face with the muck, then wipe it clean?

There was a clattering din behind me and Brom shouted, "Shit!"

Whipping my head around, I saw he'd unsettled some crumbling stones while trying to scale the wall.

"That nearly hit me in the head!" he laughed, pointing at a weighty block that was still sliding down the dirt mound at his feet. He began to climb again, then wedged himself into one of the arched windows.

Oh, Brom! I can't be healed with you bellowing curses behind me!

He doesn't matter! Dip your hand!

I stood another moment, contending with myself. Nothing seemed right.

It all looks so common. *Is this* truly *Tersewell?*

Weeds grew all around the well. The occasional call of a warbler sounded like any other bird I'd overheard whilst gathering mushrooms in Trivington Wood. No mysterious fragrance filled the air. There was nothing about the place to inspire either worship or awe, nothing other than the finely carved but broken wall, and even that was tainted by the crass fellow perched upon it.

You know *'tis Tersewell! Your expectations are unjust.*

A scrabbly thud sounded behind me. Brom had jumped down.

"Ready?" he called.

Prove your faith! Stop dithering!

"Jus-just a moment," I stuttered, staring down into the gritty water. A murky reflection glared back at me, hair hanging down both sides of its face, two blobs for eyes and a reddish smear upon its cheek.

I heard Brom slogging over the mud toward me.

"What're ya lookin' at?" He chuckled, staring at me curiously, then dropped a pebble into the water.

My reflection rippled into havoc.

"Nothing," I replied, the word heavy in my mouth.

"Let's go then." He put his hand on the curve of my waist as if to pull me away from the well.

And I let him.

***

God, forgive me.

I prayed miserably as we rejoined the road toward Thorneby.

I squandered my one chance, and all for what? To not look a fool before this fool.

I glanced at Brom as he tromped along ahead of me, scratching his head.

Have mercy on me!

"What thought you of the ruins, Madge?" Keaton asked.

Ruins. Such an apt word.

"They're a bit eerie," I said, knowing it was the wrong answer.

"Are you alright?" He stopped urging Dame along and stood, looking at me.

Before, I likely would have laughed and insisted that I was well, but at this moment, my heart was too heavy.

"I don't feel well."

"You look a bit peaked. Well, I was hoping to push on further before we stopped to camp, but if you're not well enough, we can stop sooner."

Stop sooner? That's it! But how?

"Thanks," I murmured though my mind raced.

If we're to stop, the closer the better.

261

We trudged on as diverse plans formed in my head, some quite foolish. Then, one occurred to me that shone above the others, though it too displeased me.

I'd have to lie to Keaton.

Nay. You needn't say anything.

'Twould be dishonest all the same.

Do it now. You're getting further and further away from Tersewell!

Glancing back down the road whence we'd come, I saw that the arched wall was no longer in sight. My decision was made. Slowing my pace to drop behind the others, I stepped onto a round stone embedded in the road and cried out as though jolted by pain.

Both men turned, and Keaton hurried back toward me as I sank to the ground, clutching my left foot.

"You've twisted it?" he asked, dropping down beside me.

I merely panted in response, digging my nails into my ankle to help me remember I'd chosen the left one.

I mustn't start hobbling on my right foot later.

"Might I look at it, Madge?" Keaton's eyes were worried.

I bit my lip and nodded, then wrapped my skirt around my calf and lifted my foot to him.

"It's not swelling yet. Can you try walking on it? Hey, Brom, a hand here, please."

Soon I was up, holding onto Brom's arm. Gingerly, I put my left foot out and touched my toes to the ground.

"Ohh!" I gasped, clutching wildly at Brom as if to stay upright.

"Hmm," Keaton said. "You wrenched it good, didn't you? Ugh, I'm sorry, Madge."

His eyes were concerned as his ill-founded apology burned in my ears.

"Brom, will you carry her up to that clearing there so she can rest a while?"

Putting one arm under my back and the other behind my knees, Brom easily lifted me, the bulk of his chest and arms pressing in against me.

"Clumsy girl," he murmured. His scruffy face, just inches from mine, smiled down at me as if we shared a secret.

I glanced away.

My dupery wasn't meant to wile my way into your arms, you stupid lout, I thought, hugging my arms to myself. *Ugh, and I've no right to enjoy how pleasant it feels now that I'm here.*

I tried to make myself small and very still within his hold.

Soon, I was settled upon some blankets with my back against a tree. There I stayed, plotting what I would do that night, while Brom practiced juggling and Keaton brushed out Dame's coat. After an hour or so, he asked me to stand again.

'Twas all for naught if I appear to be cured now.

I couldn't look Keaton in the eye as I rose from the ground. Once more, I feigned agony at stepping forward and was quickly lowered back down by Brom.

"Well, that's it then. Here we stay," Keaton sighed. "Perhaps we'll still get to Thorneby by tomorrow evening. I'll start collecting firewood."

You're keeping him from Jane! What else does this good man want in all the world, and you're spoiling it!

I watched him head off into the wood, knowing we were but a quarter mile from Tersewell and expecting a full moon. My prayers had been answered.

But why must the faith I need hurt others?

The Minstrel's Sense

"Madge?" Keaton's voice drifted over the dying fire from where he lay several feet away.

"Hmm?" Though I was wide awake, I responded as if I was on the brink of slumber.

"How is your ankle?"

Oh, Keaton! Please go to sleep!

"Mm...I don't know as I'm not up on it."

Since we'd all lain down after supper I'd been waiting for him to drift off. Brom had been snoring for hours, but it seemed that Keaton's keenness at seeing Jane soon kept him awake.

"Yes, of course," came his voice again. "Madge, there's something else I must say to you. I don't mean to upset you, but…"

My curiosity was genuinely piqued. "What is it?"

"Well, I've noted Brom's behavior toward you has changed in recent days."

He's seen it as well?

"What mean you?" I wondered what it looked like to him.

"He…he touches you more readily, and the way he looks at you. It's *different* now."

There's no use in pretending.

"Aye. I believe you are right."

There was an abrupt break in Brom's breathing and his body shifted under the bright moonlight. Keaton and I said nothing more until his snoring began again.

"Truly, that was my foremost concern when you first asked to travel with us – well, that and fear of your father stringing me up." He laughed, then grew somber again. "I've seen how Brom treats girls…women. If one catches his eye, he's fast and free with praise and talk, but his attentions are not longstanding. He is my friend and I am thankful for him, but he's also…"

Pappy's words came back to me. *'You've no idea what men hatch in their hearts, Daughter…We're all a bit piggish.'*

"A bit piggish?" I asked.

"Precisely," he said with a quiet chuckle. "I fear he'd debauch any girl who'd allow it. I want to keep him well away from both of my sisters. And you are dear to me as they are."

My heart warmed at this revelation. Propping up on my elbow, I peered at Keaton. His head was turned toward me, and I could make out the tender look of his face in the light from the dying fire.

"Thank you, Keaton." My gaze held his for a silent moment. "But fret not. I confess I was pleased – as well as *surprised* that I was pleased – when he called me 'pretty' yesterday, but I hear how he speaks of girls and how you speak of Jane. I'd much prefer to be a fellow's *Jane* than his *Mavis*."

"Ah, poor Mavis," he sighed. "She has her long dark locks and her dancing to commend her, but little else."

"Not even a full deck of cards now," I said, dryly.

Keaton laughed aloud, then dropped back into a whisper, "You are a clever girl, Madge. I am so very pleased that Jane shall get to meet you."

Guilt struck through my heart.

I'm hoping that you'll be going on to Jane without me.

"We ought to sleep," I told him. "You don't want to yawn as Jane greets you with a kiss."

"Mm, that I do *not*." He rolled over. "Good night, wise Madge."

"Good night, Keaton."

I lay, pondering his continual kindness toward me. He spoke truth and wisdom – such vital things! – in spite of fearing it might rile or sadden me.

He is a true friend.

And you repay him with nothing but deceit.

Stop it! What's done is done and a few added hours before he meets with Jane won't kill him.

I waited longer and finally, the slow, even breaths he took proved that exhaustion had overcome his excitement at last.

Under the cover of my blanket, I slipped my shoes on and stood. I was careful to avoid crunching any leaves or twigs as I stepped away and out of the campsite. Starting down the moon-lit and empty road, I was thankful as neither Keaton nor Brom stirred.

Wrought Me Thus

Tersewell.

Again.

The arched wall glowed majestically in the moonlight, hard and cold as I ran my hand along it. Rounding the corner, I saw the massive oak standing sentinel beside the well. Now with no Brom there to mar it, I thought the place would feel sacred. But the ground leading up to the well seemed even more mucky than before, and there was still no outburst of heavenly birdsong overhead. I stepped onto one of the well's border stones and knelt, ignoring how it bit into my knees.

Healing, at last.

Looking down into the still water, I saw the moon itself reflected there, large and round like a watchful eye.

How can I ladle up what I need and separate it from the dirt?

In the blacksmith's story, Jesus smeared mud over the blind man's eyes, so I'll spread it over my mark.

Is that right, God?

Silence.

I closed my eyes and began to pray again but stopped.

Aloud, I told myself.

Beginning once more, I spoke as reverently as I could, the sound of it breaking the near silence as the night pressed in around me.

"God, thank You I was able to return here after my failure to trust You earlier today. I humbly ask for healing of this mark that You may be glorified and that my father may look upon me without pain."

My heart pounding, I was startled by the cold of the water as I plunged my hand into the well. Digging past the sand, I found denser dirt underneath. My fingers scooped a bit up out of the water and rubbed it between my fingers. It was gritty, not the rich soil of fertile fields.

It seems very much like the dirt I oft scrub off the entryway floor, brought in by lodgers' shoes.

Stop carping! Without faith, 'tis impossible *to please God.*

I have faith, I thought, concentrating on each word as it formed in my mind.

To simply think *it proves nothing. You must* show *you have it.*

Is not leaving home and traveling here proof enough? Though why did I need to when He could heal me anywhere*? And why use mud? Would a powerful God need such elements?*

Christ used mud! 'Tis scriptural.

I shuddered, pressing a dripping hand against my temple.

Why do I have these contrary thoughts?

They are thoughts of reason.

Nay! They are arrogant, and worse – faithless. Why can I not stop them? Ugh, just carry on with it!

Taking a deep breath, I daubed the sludge onto my cheek and up over my eyelid. I scoured myself with it, picturing my flesh polished clean.

Standing upright on the flat stone, I said aloud, "I have faith that I am healed."

'Twasn't said with enough surety.

Tilting my head up toward the sky, I took a deep breath and spoke with force and clarity like Keaton each time he stepped onto a stage.

"By faith I have traveled here from afar and I am healed!"

The whole world was still around me as the thin smear began to dry and crack. I patted the crusty mask, aching for something to happen underneath it. I imagined it flaking off, taking with it bits of coarse, red flesh.

Slowly, I counted to one hundred, then knelt again to splash what little water I could onto my face, rinsing the muck away.

Ought I to touch it? If the rough flesh is still there I'll know my journey was all for naught. So, to touch it is to lack faith.

Or is it a lack of faith to not touch it?

I was unsure which thoughts were heresy as I saw sense and felt shame in all of them. My hand hovered only a moment longer.

A touch changes nothing and healed or not, I must know.

My fingers sought out where the mark had always been. The skin felt just as coarse, coarser perhaps after the scouring.

Nothing had changed.

Panic crept up on me, ready to grasp and shake me like a rabbit in a dog's jaws.

"I've come so far." I said trembling, my voice rising. "I've risked so much to stand here and be healed! Is it not enough?"

Silence.

"Must I *beg* You?"

A fury, laid hold of me, and it seemed that another person was shouting as my mouth formed words, fast and fierce.

"My own father cannot look at me because of this mark – this damn mark placed upon my cheek by *You!* By

You alone!" My throat burned as I shrieked, *"Why have You wrought me thus?"*

The treasonous question hung in the air and I sank down upon the flat stone, expecting a bolt of lightning to crack out of the night sky to destroy me.

None came.

Tears ran down my raw cheek, stinging the scratches upon it.

"Forgive me," I murmured. "I can't stem the evil in my mind. Truly, I *want* to have faith. Have mercy on me."

The words felt shameful on my tongue, but as they rang in my ears, I felt the honest cry of surrender within them.

God has wrought me thus, giving me a mind that is not lulled into thoughtless piety. I cannot change myself – not my body, nor my mind.

Gritty tears seeped into my mouth and dripped off my chin.

Marked, I am. Marked as the day of my birth. Marked, I ever shall be.

The arched wall loomed above me. Feeling heavier than I thought possible, I rose to my feet and stumbled toward it. The moon was lower now, casting less light upon the sharp ruins. I wrapped my cloak, damp with splashes of well water, more tightly around myself.

Stepping over loose rocks, I sank beside the wall, exhausted.

The faces of those who had cared for me swam before my eyes.

Keaton helped me to sing and understand myself in many ways.

Little Lulu loved me because *of my mark!*

Babs, of course, and Lottie, when her mind was still her own.

And Pappy.

"...grown difficult for me to look upon her face, such as it is."

Fresh tears formed at the memory of his words.

Nothing could have driven me from home but to hear him say such things. And yet...he did not say them to me. Had I not returned to the kitchen that night, I would be at home now, warm in my bed.

No, his words were not meant to hurt. We all have thoughts that would pain those we cherish, if given voice. How many times have I almost giggled at Keaton's awkward tottering? And yet I couldn't think more highly of him.

What meant he by "it has grown *difficult to look upon her"? The mark was there from the moment he first saw me as a baby.*

He said 'tis difficult, *but not* impossible.

The vast abbey grounds yawned around me, so very empty and still. There was the graveyard, its countless headstones nearly glowing in the dark. I wondered at the souls who'd been buried there in years past, sorry that nary a one remained to haunt me in that moment of abysmal solitude.

My mark only separated me from people when I fled them to be healed of it.

A breeze, chillier than before, made my loose tresses dance before my eyes. The wall's stones dug into my back, drawing heat from my flesh and bones. I remembered Keaton's question.

"Do they all run their separate ways to hide and shiver alone until dawn?"

The loneliness I had always felt tugging at my elbow, wrapped itself around my head, forcing its way into my mouth and down my throat to lay, sour and heavy, in my gut.

I know not what lizards do, but I know I will not stay here alone.

Rising to my feet in the moonlight, I stepped carefully across the broken, jumbled paving stones, the arches soaring above me into the night sky. Through the silent graveyard I trod to the rutted lane that led to the road back to camp.

275

Asking Such Things

The sky was just beginning to lighten as I stepped into camp. Still, I had not arrived before Keaton was up. Just the sight of his misshapen body seated next to the fire ring as he dropped kindling into it heartened me. Yet, I wondered what I would say to him and I stepped forward shyly.

Catching sight of me, he stopped stirring the ashes and with a look of wonder on his face, asked, "You're healed?"

I froze in midstep.

Healed?

Slowly, my hand began to reach toward my face.

It did *work?*

"Your ankle..." he said. "It feels well this morning?"

Oh...

"Yes," I nodded, my heart thumping wildly. "'Tis sound enough."

Stretching out my leg, I showed him how I could move my ankle this way and that.

"Miraculous!" He smiled broadly, looked from my empty blankets to the road, growing puzzled. "I woke and saw your bed empty. Where were you?"

Looking at my face again, he seemed embarrassed. "And why are you...so dirty?"

I gazed at him, steadily, silently.

Please don't ask me such things, Keaton.

My silent plea was joined by tears welling in my eyes.

He grew grave as he watched them slip down my cheeks.

Glancing down the road toward Tersewell, he beckoned me toward the fire, now lively with flames. "Never mind, Madge. I won't pry. Please don't cry."

He patted the ground next to him and I settled myself there, drying my face.

After a quiet moment, he laid his hand over mine and murmured, "My father took me there when I was a child."

I stopped breathing.

"...dipped me into the well up to my neck."

Squeezing his hand, I laid my head on his shoulder.

"It didn't work for me, either."

He began to chuckle.

"…quite obviously."

Startled, I struggled to think of a reply. But then, I giggled.

Our amusement grew and we laughed together, my head bouncing atop his shoulder. My body ached with weariness, but the contentment I felt in that moment was immeasurable. Once our humor was spent, we sat quietly for a while, gazing into the fire until I lifted my head and spoke.

"I'm heading home today."

"What?" He looked alarmed. "But we're off to Thorneby! I can't…I can't take you back to Trivington just yet."

"Nay! You go home to Sweet Jane. I shall go by coach."

"Ah, aye. I knew the money you earned could serve you well," he said pointedly.

Looking into his eyes, I was struck with how keenly I would miss him.

"Keaton," I said, a lump rising in my throat. "You are the dearest friend I've ever had."

He leaned his forehead against mine. "And I wish I could call you 'sister', Madge. But I shall have to content myself with visiting you and Babs and Lottie but once or twice a summer. In the meantime…"

Here he lumbered to a standing position.

"...if we are to get you to Spirely in time to board the coach, we ought to awaken Smells Aplenty and go now."

"Good bye, dear Dame," I whispered into her ear. It flicked at my words, softly batting my nose. Looking into her large and long-lashed eyes, I rubbed her neck, pleased that God had thought to form such a gentle, steadfast creature.

Having just paid my coach fare, I was now standing alongside Spirely's High Street with Keaton and Brom. Boarding was at noon, which left me an hour or so to seek out a meal for my rumbling stomach.

Having said my goodbyes to Keaton, and now Dame, I turned to Brom. He was looking around, as if searching for something out in the bustle of the street.

"Thank you for your company and encouragement, Brom," I said, realizing my words were surprisingly apt.

"Yeah, alright Madge," he said, halting his search long enough to look me in the eye. "I'll see ya again should we come through Trivington. And ale's there at yer place, yeah?"

"Uh…yeah, I'm certain we'll still be serving ale at the Gander's Wing next summer."

What an odd question! But, this is Brom…

"Good bye, good fellow." I leaned forward to hug him in parting, once again catching a whiff of his sweaty body.

He looked surprised, then patted my back awkwardly. "G'bye. Hey, Keat – I'm goin' ta see if Nelly's still workin' at the Unicorn. What say we meet up outside of Thorneby in two days' time? Yeah?"

"Umm, very well," Keaton replied, his brow creasing. "I'll see you there."

"'Right then."

With that, the first fellow to ever call me *pretty* walked off down the street without another look back, his pack dangling from his shoulder, his steps sprightly.

"Well, Keaton, your worries were well-founded," I said, gravely. "Clearly he loved me truly and is heartbroken at my departure."

"Ha ha! Perhaps this Nelly will salve his anguish." Keaton's laughter rang out, then he shook his head. "Poor fool. Madge, are you sure you wouldn't like me to stay until the coach comes?"

"I couldn't keep you from Jane another moment." I leaned in to hug him.

"Oh, how I regret you won't meet her!" he said, wrapping his long arms around me one last time.

Yes, his remarkable Rose of Thorneby shall remain a mystery to me.

"As do I. Now go! Run to her!"

"I shall take great delight in doing so!" He grinned, then bowed. "God keep you, Madge."

"And you, my friend."

He pulled the mule around and headed off, prompting her with, "Step high, Dame! 'Twill be your own stable tonight!"

I leaned against a hitching post, weary and hungering, watching until he was out of sight.

Thank You for that remarkable little minstrel. And now, to feed my belly.

Standing on the corner, I saw three pubs nearby, but the scent of roast beef and onions pulled me inside the dim, low-ceilinged dining room of the one called the Crimson Lion.

Though I had combed my hair, and washed my face since my nighttime wanderings, I knew I looked travel-worn. Many times, bedraggled travelers had wandered into the Gander's dining room, looking as if they wouldn't have the money to pay for their fare, but Pappy had taught me otherwise.

"Being long on these English roads can take a toll on anyone – turn a duke into a lout, a princess into a drab. 'Tis best, though, to see their money before putting a plate in front of them."

With this in mind, I had already dug a coin out of my knotted handkerchief and laid it immediately down on the table where I wearily settled myself.

A heavy young woman wearing an apron approached, eyeing the coin on the table.

"What would ya like, my sweet?" she asked, smiling, a pretty dimple in her cheek.

Moments later, I was urging myself *not* to lick the plate clean. The savory meal had been delicious and the swirls of gravy left behind begged to follow it down my throat.

Sorry Babs, but the Lion's roast has bested yours.

With the fullness of my belly, I was beset by a wave of fatigue and my head and limbs felt like lead.

At times, guests would fall asleep in the Gander's dining hall once their plates were empty. If the table wasn't needed, we'd leave them be for a spell, snickering if their mouths dropped open to rattle with snoring.

Resting my head against the back of the bench, I decided to close my eyes for a few moments.

But I shall sleep tonight, not before, as I've a coach to board.

For More Ceruse

As I stepped up to the entrance of the Gander's Wing, a voice drifted down to me from the upper story. Its words were vague, as if spoken through water, but grew clearer as the front door swung open at my touch.

"You're quite tired, aren't you?" it said.

I thought the question odd and wondered what was bumping my elbow. The door vanished and my eyelids, heavy as full tankards, lifted slowly. Before me was a dirty plate on a table.

I was still in the Crimson Lion.

"And far from home," the voice continued, smooth as warm oil.

Groggily, I turned to see who spoke.

"Why are you not at *your* inn?"

A man stood beside my table.

"Never mind. I will allow you your secrets."

"Pardon me?" I asked, my lips sluggish with the effort.

He was well dressed, well spoken, neither young nor old.

"It appears that you've no more of the gift I left you."

"Gift?" I asked, waking further.

Who is this strange fellow?

As he tilted his head to examine me, I remembered and sat up straight.

The Smirking Sod.

"Why the ceruse, of course." He gibed. "Did you not get it? Perhaps the other woman – she with the eel pie – took it. Ha! To think such a hag would bother! Rest assured, I intended it for *you,* the ceruse *and* the money."

'Twas you *who left those? Not the Little Wife?*

"That was less than a fortnight past! I thought 'twould last you longer. Fear not. You shall have more." He winked and reached for the purple coin purse at his belt. "The apothecary there by the bakery must sell it."

He opened the little sack and pulled a coin from its depths. He held it out, the sunlight through the window glinting off its hard, gold surface.

"No, than…" I stopped myself.

I've naught to thank *him for!*

"No?" He tilted his head again, pouting playfully. "I thought a girl such as yourself would like some help with her complexion. You've such potential."

He reached out with his empty hand as if to touch my face.

Recoiling, I shook my head and looked away, trapped by the table before me and his body beside it.

"Come now. Don't be coy." He moved toward me, lowering his voice in a way that made my shoulders hunch forward. "This coin could do much good for you and is but a trifle to me."

I stared hard at the table as he lowered himself to sit beside me. His hip pressed against mine as if to slide me along the bench. I gripped the table with both hands and wedged my feet against its heavy legs.

"Go buy your wife a comb," I snarled, "Before her hair falls out."

"What?" he asked, all mirth and slyness fled from his voice. His side no longer pressed against mine.

I answered nothing, my heart beating furiously.

He made a little sound of disgust and stood up straight.

"Stupid bitch."

He flung the coin at me, pelting my head and I heard him walk away, his shoes clicking on the wooden floor. I watched as the coin slid off my lap to the floor where it rolled to a stop against my shoe.

Someone will find that there and be very glad of it.

I stared at it a little longer, allowing the man plenty of time to get far away, then stood, hoisting my pack to my shoulder.

With my head held high, I was walking out the Lion's door before it occurred to me that I may have slept through the coach's boarding time.

Kicking Rocks

I trod down the wooded road fuming, the strap of my pack digging into my shoulder. When I discovered the coach had left without me, I decided to start walking toward Spirely. I needed to get there by evening so I could board another coach first thing the following morning. I'd made good progress, but I wasn't sure it was enough as I ached with exhaustion.

Stopping for a moment at the top of a hill, I looked down into the glen below. The trees were thinner there and a stream, silver in the sunlight, snaked through its trough.

At least this looks familiar.

I'd already passed the Quakers' meeting house, shuttered and dark, it being Saturday.

Tomorrow, 'twill be full of Friends, its door open to admit any and all into its silent center.

I rued there were no Friends there now, as I was sure one of them would allow me a ride in their carriage or wagon that I might rest my weary body.

Many other travelers, mostly on horseback, journeyed alongside me, but I kept my head down and my pace as quick as fatigue would allow. I was thankful for the coins Keaton had refused to accept as they would buy me a bed at an inn that night.

I'll make certain tomorrow's coach doesn't leave me behind. Oh, to lie upon a bed...

Soon, I passed where we had slept the night we'd met Thrin.

That's where I first made fire.

The ring of blackened stones was still in the same spot. Stepping off the road, I walked through the campsite and into the woods to relieve myself. As I crouched in the midst of the bracken, the sound of singing, very poor singing, drifted to my ears.

Too much ale fuels that lyric, I thought as a line was repeated again and again. *And I've no interest in meeting with him who sings it.*

I froze in place, listening as the drunkard drew nearer. Under his song was the steady, rhythmic thud of hooves riding past. Once the dreadful melody had faded considerably, I dared to peek out from amongst the fronds.

Just before he disappeared down the road, I saw that the sot was a large man, clinging with both arms to a pony's neck. He looked as if he might at any moment slide off the beast's back into a sloppy heap upon the ground. His bellowing mouth was just inches from his steed's ear.

Poor pony, on many counts.

Once he was out of sight and earshot, I stood and hastened down the road, hopeful I would not overtake him as we traveled in the same direction. Treading onward, I sighed.

Perhaps Keaton has his arms wrapped around his sweetheart at this very moment.

I smiled, remembering how his eyes twinkled whenever Jane's name was mentioned. It cheered me to know that not all girls my age were as spiteful as Mavis or as chafing as Thrin.

Certainly, some good young women live upon the earth.

The Little Wife could smile in spite of being wed to a swine. She might make the best of friends. Where was she today? Perhaps they're not even married and he discarded her after his vile attentions.

My heart ached, hoping she wasn't alone somewhere.

If her husband cast her off, would her father want her to come home?

I stopped suddenly in the road, struck by a horrible thought.

Does Pappy *want* me *back?*

Certainly, he wanted me back at first, but I left at our busiest time of year! As time passed and he had to run the Gander with only Babs to help him, maybe...

Nay! Pappy truly loves me and I have faith he wants me home. Can an honest faith such as this please God? Though selfish, 'tis the only sort I'm able to muster.

Pondering this, I rounded a bend and saw twenty feet before me in the road, a woman and a man. They were face to face, speaking to one another, but the sound of the nearby stream drowned out their words. By them stood a pony, pawing the ground.

I glanced around, seeking a route that I might avoid them, but the narrowest part of the brook went right past them. I was unwilling to cross higher or lower and come away with a wet skirt and shoes so I took a few steps closer to the couple. Meaning just to hurry by, it was a moment before I realized whom was before me.

Thrin?

Oh, of course! She's headed toward the campsite to sleep before Meeting on the morrow.

I stifled a smile, wondering, *What is she chiding him about?*

But then I saw she was wringing her hands together and leaning back, away from the man.

Who is he?

He stuck a finger out at her and swayed slightly on his feet as his pony's reins slipped from his other hand.

My heart sank.

The drunken singer!

Neither had yet noticed me though I was now close enough to hear their words as he took a stumbling step toward her.

"I seen ya walkin' through here ev'ry Saturd'y." The man leaned forward. "So's I thought 'twould only be right fer me ta stop an' say hello."

"Hel...hello to thee," Thrin replied, then attempted to step past him.

"Ah, nay. That's not all!" He said, shaking his head and finger, then began to laugh. "God, I'm dizzy! Yer beauty's spinnin' me head!"

As if to steady himself, he grabbed onto her shoulder with one hand and clutched his forehead with the other. The sudden touch awoke something within Thrin, and she shrieked, pushing at the man. His pony stepped about uneasily.

"Now, now, none o' that!" The man said, his grip on her arm enduring. "Ya got...ya got the wrong idea. I jes' wanted..."

He didn't finish saying what he wanted, instead pulling her closer to him.

"Jesus!" Thrin screamed, her face in complete terror, her arms flailing.

"Oh, heh heh," the man laughed. "I ain't Him!"

Frantically looking around, I saw there was no one is sight. Though there had been a steady stream of horsemen and amblers along the road earlier, none of them were now near.

Oh, God. It's me! Just me!

My heart racing, I stooped to pick up a large stick and stepped closer to the couple.

Even shriller, Thrin cried out again, "Jesus!"

Go!

I flew toward them, hollering, "Nay!"

The man turned with a look of such sluggish surprise that I would've laughed if I hadn't been so terribly frightened.

He still gripped Thrin's arm, but stepped away just enough to face me as I closed in.

"Wha...what are ya...where'd ya come from?" he sputtered.

Thrin whimpered, struggling to get out of the man's grasp.

"Let her go!" I said, waving the stick at his face. The drunkard watched it pass, his eyes crossing with the effort, then curled his lip into a snarl.

The image of Pappy holding a pillow while bellowing at me filled my mind.

'Break his hinddanglers, Madgie!'

Squaring my stance, I aimed a kick at the man's crotch, but the toe of my shoe bounced off the inside of his thigh.

In slow response, the man looked down toward his legs and turned his knees in, as if to guard the area.

'Aaaand again!'

I swung my leg at him once more with a force that would have pleased Pappy heartily. My foot sank into the spot sought and the man doubled over with a yowl, releasing Thrin. Stumbling backward, he fell into the shallow stream with a splash.

"Ohh...me rocks," he moaned, his hands clutching at his danglers. "A woods witch has gone and...and kicked me poor, poor rocks."

Though he looked and sounded completely helpless, I recalled Pappy's urging that an angered man was a fearsome foe.

Though I'd never struck an animal before, I lifted the stick and swung it at the pony's round haunches. There was a smack I was loath to hear and the pony galloped off down the road, neighing.

Turning, I saw that Thrin's eyes were nearly as wide as her mouth as she gazed at me in wonder.

"Whence came thee?" she asked.

"Come *on!*" I grabbed her wrist and pulled her so hard she nearly fell down.

We left the road, fleeing into the woods, me ahead, Thrin behind. On and on we ran, skirting past brush and fallen branches, until I felt my throbbing heart might burst through my chest.

Just a little farther, I told myself.

I knew the pony had galloped a ways off, and even if it returned, I supposed that the man's throbbing danglers would make him averse to straddling anything.

Still, we are far from town, and now we're off the road entirely!

Slowing just a little, I suddenly heard a strange noise. Thinking Thrin was weeping from fear, I slowed further and turned to look.

She wasn't crying. She was laughing.

With her eyes squeezed shut, laughter poured out of her mouth as her legs carried her forward. Never having heard so much as a mild giggle out of her before, I stopped and stared. Tears ran down her cheeks which were rounded and pink with hilarity.

"What is it?" I asked, dreading that she may have lost her mind.

"Oh, Madge!" Thrin began, coughing as she spoke the words. "When I called out to Jesus, *thou* appeared and…and…" She clutched her belly with her free hand, her shoulders quivering.

I asked, "And he thought I was a *woods witch*?"

"Yes! And..." She gasped for air, wiping her eyes. "And..."

The corners of my mouth twitched. "And I *kicked* him?"

"Oh," Thrin said, the smile suddenly dropping from her face though tears still filled her eyes. "Oh, I oughtn't laugh at *that*."

Worry lines creased her forehead and her voice, solemn now, said, "We ought never to hurt another, mean they ill or well."

Ugh, here comes the sermon!

Wishing I'd said nothing, I started forward again through the woods, pulling her along. But the lecture didn't come. Instead, she began to weep.

Glancing over my shoulder, I saw how miserably she stumbled along, towed ever forward by my grasp. Her cries grew more fervent until a great peal of sobbing lifted from her body into the tree branches above us.

"Thrin!" I spun around and yanked her arm, whispering fiercely, "He might hear you! We must get out of these woods, and you *must* stop blubbing!"

Her weeping quieted to sniffling as we shambled on. After a while, the woods opened up and we stepped out onto the edge of a bluff, able to view fields and, in the far distance, a very large town.

Spirely?

My heart lifted.

Did cutting through the woods shorten my way there? But first, I must get Thrin home.

"Which way to your farm?" I asked her firmly.

Her red-rimmed eyes scanned the land as she sniffed again.

"There," she said softly, pointing toward the north. Then she asked, her voice woefully small, "Madge, what would he have done had thou not kicked him?"

She looked so sad and uncertain, so unlike herself, that I stopped gripping her wrist and held her hand instead.

"I don't know, Thrin."

She was silent for a moment. "Well, I don't think 'twas right of thee…"

Ugh! Here is the Thrin I know.

I bit my lip, waiting for the reproof sure to follow and recalling the uselessness of gainsaying her.

"…but I thank thee for doing so."

What did she just say?

I stopped walking and watched her tear-streaked face in wonder. She was calm now. Her face looked neither frightened, nor assured, but wistful. After a deep sigh, she murmured, "At times, I don't know what the Inward Light has said or wants from me."

The weight of her words settled into my heart as I stared at her forlorn, blotchy face. Then I wrapped my arms around her.

"Me neither," I whispered.

She lifted her arms to encircle me as well. Quietly, we stood on the edge of the forest, holding each other. After several moments, she pulled away, dried her eyes, and grabbed my hand.

"The farm is this way."

***

The surprising change in Thrin was short-lived.

As we approached the drive leading to her home, she said in a voice as lordly as ever, "We needn't mention to my parents what happened in the woods just now. They would only chide me, telling me that's what comes of 'turning Quaker'."

"Perhaps not what comes of turning Quaker, but rather what comes of traveling through the forest alone," I said, noting how *she* was now pulling *me* by the hand.

"Well, they'd likely blame it on my convictions, so we won't be saying anything of it to them, alright?" Her eyes delved into mine, exacting an answer.

"Oh, well, I shan't be saying *anything* to them at all." To the east I saw the lofty steeples of Spirely's many churches piercing the sky. "I must make it to town before dark."

"Oh," she said, sounding disappointed. Her hand tightened around mine. "I thought thou would stay the night."

"Thank you, but I've got to board the coach to Trivington early on the morrow, so this is goodbye."

"Well then..." she dropped my hand and smoothed her hair back from her face. "I must tell thee...I was truly frightened, and umm, said some things I did not mean, and I..."

Nay! Don't slip back into that!

"Thrin," I interrupted. "Not all thoughts and feelings that disquiet us are evil. Allow yourself to know them."

"What?" The puzzled look on her face was fleeting, replaced with one of knowing. She sighed, looking as if her patience was being tried. "I mean no disrespect to thee, Madge, but the *Inward Light* is the One Who directs me as to what is proper, not thou."

I stifled a sigh of my own. *I cannot teach you here and now what I have just learned for myself. You must live your own story, dear girl.*

My heart softened toward her as I imagined what that might look like.

"Yes, Thrin. I believe you are right. I must go now." I leaned in to embrace her stiff shoulders. "Good bye."

"I shall pray for thee," she called out as I started off.

I merely waved as I took my last leave of her, thinking, *And I shall for you, as well.*

.

An Even Trade

"Wexhall!"

We'd gone through three towns already that morning, but every time the coachman hollered out in his gruff, bellowing voice, it jarred me again.

Though I'd stayed at a reasonably comfortable inn the night before, my sleep had been fitful as I'd worried about missing the early morning departure.

A child seated beside me, pulled back the curtain to watch as we careened past the crowded buildings lining Wexhall's High Street. The rest of his family sat opposite us, chatting happily amongst themselves the entire journey. I'd heard they were disembarking at Wexhall, so unless someone else boarded there, I'd have the coach to myself all the way to Trivington.

The coach pulled to an abrupt halt, nearly unseating me and the coachman shouted out again.

"Respite and horse-change!"

The door swung open and my fellow travelers descended the step to the street below. I was last to climb out into the bright sunlight, my back aching, my throat dry. Stretching all of my limbs, I looked around, seeking a shady spot to pass the time as the spent horses were exchanged for fresh ones.

This coach will not be leaving without me. I've paid fare to Trivington and I intend to ride all the way there.

The air was thick with dust, stirred up by the bustling traffic. People crowded the walkways along the storefronts, calling out, some selling wares, others greeting friends.

"Cold ale!"

"Margaret!"

A water well, between two inns and surrounded by a clump of trees beckoned to me.

From there, I shall be able to watch the coach while filling up my waterskin.

A stableman was leading the tired horses away as I turned the windlass to bring the bucket back up. I leaned over the well's edge and saw the water's surface several feet down. My reflection was there, small and wavering.

'What there thou seest, fair creature, is thyself.' The words of Milton filled my head as I gazed at my rippling image below.

I'm not returning home the way I wanted, the way I'd hoped.

The dripping bucket was heavy, ungainly in my hands as I attempted to fill the skin through its narrow opening.

What am I to say to Pappy? Oh drat! I've spilled half of it!

"Might I help you?" a deep voice said as a pair of hands grasped the bucket.

I looked up and gasped.

Yates.

"'*Tis* you!" he said, taking the bucket from me. "I saw the coach coming down High Street and stopped, not truly expecting to see *you* climb out! But when you did, I called out but you didn't turn so I thought maybe '*twasn't* you, and I…"

He fell silent and we looked at each other for a moment, both dazed. I forced myself to hold his gaze.

Don't drop your head like Peggy.

"Oh," he said quietly, shifting his eyes to my left cheek. "You're scratched."

My eyes *did* flit away at that.

Yes, that's what happens when you scour your face with dirt.

I felt his eyes upon my mark which was blighted further by my efforts to remove it and wondered what he was thinking.

He seems to have no difficulty gazing upon it, unlike Pappy.

As if privy to my thoughts, he dropped the bucket back into the well and said softly, "I've a message from your father."

"What is it?" My eyes stung with sudden tears.

Yates glanced around. "He said he wants you home no matter what's happened and he loves you beyond anything."

Wants me home.

A little sob escaped my throat as a teardrop fell from my lashes.

Yates bit his lip, looking solemn.

No matter what's happened.

A peace descended upon me though more tears slid down my face.

"Please. Come, sit." Yates put his hand on my shoulder and led me to a patch of grass under the trees. As we lowered ourselves to the ground, he said, "Each time we meet, it seems I either frighten or upset you."

He thinks I shirk and quake at everything.

"Nay," I sniffed and smiled, daubing my nose with my sleeve. "You've gladdened me, truly."

"Here." Lifting a flap on his pack, he pulled out a bundle of swaths. Most looked to be leather, but he found a scrap of thin cloth and handed it to me. It was soft against my cheeks and lip.

"Thank you," I murmured. Thankful for the distraction, I asked, "What are those?"

"Remnants," he said, rebinding the pile. "All *clean*, I might add. I collect every scrap I'm able to. That's what I fashioned your shoes from, trying to match up the best bits of leather together. Did your father let you – Oh! You've got them on now."

He smiled broadly, laying the bundle aside to lean over my outstretched leg and inspect my foot.

"Why are you in Wexhall, today?" I asked, resettling my skirt, wondering how much of my bare ankle he'd just seen.

"Hodges needed a new set of awls and there weren't any to be had anywhere closer to Trivington." He said this all over his shoulder, still inspecting my shoes.

I snickered as never in my life had a person hovered over my feet in such a manner.

"But, I've got them now." He patted his pack. "So I'm back to the shop by nightfall."

Across the inn's yard, I saw the stableman leading a different pair of horses toward the front of the coach.

Oh, nay! I've so many questions for him still!

"Yates," I said, frantically forming a plan. "I need to reboard now, but I'd like to pay your fare that you might join me."

"Pay my fare?" He sat up and looked at me, surprised. "Nay. I always walk."

I stood, reaching into my bodice for the handkerchief of coins. The weight of it assured me I could cover the cost as I'd offered.

"Please! I'd like to talk with you more, and…and you made me a *pair of shoes*!" I exclaimed, beckoning him toward the coach. "We'll call it an even trade."

Jumping to his feet, he started after me, his pack dangling from his shoulder.

"But that's a lot of money. I…I couldn't let you…"

I held a coin out to the coachman who was lounging against the door. "Another passenger to Trivington, please."

He glanced at Yates, shrugged and dropped the money into his pocket. "Alright."

"There! It's paid," I said brightly to Yates. "Now you have no choice."

Though his mouth was still working in silent protestation, he followed me through the coach's door.

Settling myself upon the seat, I felt a wave of relief.

I'm coming, Pappy.

Yates sat opposite me, upright as if it pained him to lean back against the seat. In spite of this, he was a fine-looking fellow, I realized as I studied him.

Not quite handsome, but pleasant looking. That blue tunic is the first thing I noticed about him. Clearly it doesn't enshroud as manly a figure as Brom's, but he's just feet away and I've yet to catch a whiff of anything unpleasant.

There was a jangle of horses' reins and the coach jolted to a start. Yates glanced around as if trying to understand how he came to be sitting there.

Poor fellow. I nearly giggled. *I must put him at ease.*

"Where is your dog today?"

"Oh!" he replied. "Hare isn't *mine*. He's Hodges's. But he follows me constantly, then runs off so it seems to everyone that I've lost him." He chuckled and settled back in the seat as the coach pulled forward. "Once he trailed me all the way to Carfmore, plaguesome little creature."

I laughed, perhaps louder than was warranted, pleased to see him relaxing.

"Might I look at your shoes again?" he asked.

Still thinking about my footwear, are you? I suppressed a smile as I slipped them off to hand over, hoping they didn't smell.

"Ugh," he said, pointing at a seam. "I don't like how those pieces come together. No wonder Hodges laughed at them. I almost didn't give them to you. Are they comfortable, at the least?"

His eyes were hopeful.

"Oh, very!"

"I've just started to learn how to fashion wooden soles, so I had to make these entirely of leather." There was no teasing in his voice as he asked, "Can you feel little stones underfoot whilst running through the woods?"

In spite of my complete embarrassment at how we'd first met, I burst out laughing. "How often do you think I *run* through the woods? It happened but once!"

Well, twice, I thought, recalling how I'd pulled Thrin along through the trees just the day before. *And the shoes served me quite well that second time.*

His face mischievous, he asked, "Do you often *sing* in the woods?"

I bit my lip. "At times."

"Well, I was very pleased to hear it, actually glad for once that Hare had run off."

Hmm. How many times have I pleasantly recalled the marveling look his face held that day?

"And I truly am sorry that I frightened you as I did. I promise I wasn't *spying* on you."

My face grew hot, but I laughed.

"Well, I *did* spy on you when you came to the inn. Can you forgive me?" I smiled at my hands, clutched together in my lap.

Look him in the eye.

Lifting my head, I saw him nod with a lop-sided smile, his large, brown eyes never wavering from my face. I felt they were admiring me as Babs's voice echoed in my mind.

"In time, teeth fall out, and muscles wilt, so the man who woos with his eyes, woos longest."

Yes, Yates's eyes are very fine indeed. But that's not all there is to him.

I thought of the hours he spent making me shoes, and his willingness to face Pappy while delivering them.

Pappy...

"Yates, why did my father give *you* that message for me?"

"Well, when I told him I was off to Wexhall, he asked me to keep an eye out for you."

I tilted my head, confused. "How knew he I might be here?"

"The wax seal from the letter you sent. He recognized it as coming from the home of a great family here in Wexhall. He inquired after you there last week."

Pappy went searching for me?

Looking away, he quietly added, "All they could tell him was that you were traveling with a minstrel."

Oh, yes that is what they would say! What must Yates think of me? What must Pappy think of me?

"Well, that sounds very different from how it actually was. That is, I *was* traveling with a minstrel, but I..."

Yates looked at me again.

"Well, it's...it's not as if I ran off just to be with the minstrel." My voice shook with embarrassed laughter.

'Twas the juggler who made my heart flutter. Ugh. I shan't ever tell anyone that part of my story!

Yates surprised me with a laugh. "That's good for the minstrel, I suppose as your father seemed set on murder when you disappeared! He stormed into our shop bellowing, 'What have you done with my bloody daughter?' Nearly stopped my heart when I saw 'twas *me* he was asking!"

"What?" I gasped.

"I swore I knew nothing of your whereabouts, sputtering all the while. 'Twasn't the finest speech ever delivered but looking back I'm rather proud I was able to speak at all. He was purple and fit to burst, about to lunge over the counter at me!"

I could picture it all so clearly, I laughed along with him though it troubled me knowing Pappy had been so upset.

But I'm on my way now to make it right.

"It took Hodges and Bill both to convince him I'd been in the shop all week, never gone long enough to nab a girl, willing or otherwise." His laughter cut off and he cleared his throat, glancing at me uneasily. "Sorry for how that sounded."

I shook my head, smiling. "I'm sorry he nearly killed you. He's truly a very kind man."

"Yes," he nodded. "He hasn't so much as shaken his fist at me in days."

I noted the stubble surrounding his wry smile.

"Pappy's keeping company with you now, is he?"

His voice grew serious. "Well, I've gone to the inn each evening to ask if he had any news of you...Margaret?"

'I'm called Madge', I nearly said, but caught myself. *I rather like that he calls me something different. I feel as if I am different.*

Wetting my lips, I pushed my hair back, looked him in the eye and asked, "Yes?"

His eyes were filled with concern. "Why *did* you run off? I was much troubled to hear of it."

I took a deep breath and thought of his merry laugh whilst speaking of Pappy about to throttle him, his trekking across Trivington each night to ask after me.

I could answer your question, Yates, at least in part, but...

"That tangled tale is not yet complete." I said, solemnly. "But soon I'll be back at the Gander and it shall be."

A smile broke over his face. "Might I visit you there?"

"Yes, I should like that very much."

An appreciative glow warmed his eyes as they rested on my face.

And perhaps someday I shall tell you all *of my story, Yates of Lethwood.*

"And now," I said. "Tell me of Lethwood."

Under the Wing

Home.

Yates was still speaking, had been since we climbed off the coach at Water Street, but all of his words blurred into gibberish as the Gander came into view.

The new sign hanging above the front entrance still looked foreign to me. The dog rose canes were overgrown, heavy with blooms and hanging sloppily, partially blocking the front door.

Those need a trim. It's not like Pappy to neglect the front entrance like this.

The thought panged me as I turned to the left and walked toward the kitchen.

"Well, I suppose I ought to take my leave of you," Yates said. "Margaret, may I come by tomorrow evening that we might talk some more?"

"Hm?" My hand paused on the door handle as I looked at him, remembering he was there and realizing that his being there pleased me. "Yes, Yates. And thank you for coming with me from Wexhall. See you tomorrow."

We gazed at each other for an instant.

You *seem to enjoy looking upon my face. 'Tis a relief that* someone *does.*

Then he bobbed his head and turned to go.

Taking a deep breath, I pulled the handle and stepped through the door. My eyes had not adjusted to the comparative indoor gloom before I heard a yelp and felt Babs's strong, fleshy hands upon me.

"You're well!" she sputtered, grasping my arms. "You're alive and here!"

I choked on laughter, struggling in her relentless clutch, dropping my pack and blankets to the floor. Pulling away, my arms were sticky with bread dough.

"Oh, sorry!" Babs said, stepping back from the embrace to stare tearfully at my face.

"No, I'm not!" she reconsidered and pulled me back into her arms, using her doughy fingers to push my hair back. Muffling a sob, she planted a wet kiss on the left side of my face.

Lottie was in her corner, asleep in spite of the noise we were making.

"Where have you..." Babs began to ask, then cut herself off. "Has your father seen you?"

"Nay."

"We must find him!" she said, looping her arm through mine and dragging me toward the hallway. "He's past dead with worry!"

316

"Babs?" I said. "Babs! I am very glad to see you, more than you know, but I must go to him alone."

A look of shock flitted across her face, then was replaced with the familiar stolid look I was used to. "Oh, of course. Sorry about the mess I've made of you."

I looked down to see the bodice of my dress dusted with flour as she reached to pull off little blobs of dough that were drying on my face.

"It's good to be home," I said, leaning forward to rest my forehead against her own and stare into her eyes. "Now where might Pappy be?"

"Well, he's likely in the front entry, sitting on the finest chair, staring at nothing. That's where he was this morning and late last night," Babs replied. "Though he may have gone off again to holler for you in the woods.

"Here," she continued, grabbing a plate that held half an apple tart. "Take him that. He's not eaten since you disappeared."

My heart sank at her words. Holding the plate, I pushed through the swinging door to stand in the hallway beyond.

Here, I thought, staring at the spot where I'd sunk to the floor just over a week earlier. *This is where I heard it. 'It has grown difficult for me to look upon her face, such as it is.'*

The lift and fall of his voice in those words would stay with me forever.

And now, I will go to him. But what shall I say?

Though I had feverishly considered this from the time of my dark night in the abbey ruins, I had settled on nothing.

I began to walk down the hall to the entryway, the thump of my heart filling my throat and ears as I neared the front desk.

'Tis so very quiet. Maybe he is not here.

The long handle of the entry bell stood upright on the desk's surface. I longed to reach for and ring it, its clear ting hanging in the air of the still room, summoning Pappy. Not an overwrought Pappy, but the happy, wonted one who was always pleased to hear the bell and greet a guest.

Just then, I saw him just as Babs said I might, in the chair gazing into emptiness. His lank hair was messy upon his head, and the flesh of his face hung loosely under his eyes and along his jaw as if he'd aged ten years in less than a fortnight. I was struck to the heart and my eyes filled with tears.

Look at what I've done to him.

He didn't stir at my approach.

Surely, he heard me creep in. The floorboards gave me away.

I stepped closer and watched as he ran a hand up over his face and through his hair, still staring at nothing. Holding the plate before me, I stopped five feet from him.

"I've still no hunger, Babs," he muttered, waving a hand in my direction.

"Please..." I began, then stopped.

"I'm telling you..." Pappy sounded angry as he finally turned toward me. His glare dropped into a look of disbelief.

"S...Sarah?" Then he leapt from the chair to nearly tackle me, shouting, "My God! Madgie! You're here!"

Weeping, he continued, "I thought you were your mother just now. Thought I'd gone and truly lost my mind! But you're here! Where'd you go, Madgie?"

He was blubbering now, the words fighting their way out of his sputtering, wet mouth. "Why'd you leave me? I couldn't bear it! Why'd you go?"

He felt unsteady on his feet as he crushed me in his arms. I held his swaying body, my cheek against his.

Tell him. Now.

"Shh, Pappy," I tried to croon though my voice caught in my throat. I wondered if he'd even hear me over his weeping.

"I must tell you something. Pappy, you *must* listen."

His blubbering slowed to gentle sobs and I pressed my mouth to his ear.

"Though it pains you to see my mark, it is a part of me and I cannot bear to have you forever looking away from it."

"What?" he asked, pulling away just a bit, then roughly pushing my hair back off my face. The plate was on the floor between us and bits of the squashed tart fell from our clothing.

I forced myself to stare back at him, my mark burning like fire on my cheek.

"Pappy, I heard what you said the night Yates brought the shoes…about my birthmark."

He looked as confused as before and shook his head slightly. "Your mark?"

"You and Babs were in the kitchen and thought I'd gone to bed and you told her it had become difficult for you to…to look upon my face, such as it is."

Realization dawned on his grizzled, sagging face.

"Nay, Madgie! Nay!" He pulled me close again. "'Twasn't your *mark* I spoke of. As you've grown, your face is more and more like your mother's. When I see you smile, it's as if my Sarah's alive again, living and breathing before me. That alone is what pains me though it pleases me."

The meaning of his words sank in, at which I wept for both joy and sorrow.

How stupid, I've been! I could have been lost to him forever, all because I listened at the door and knew not what I heard.

"Forgive me," I whispered. "I should have trusted in your love for me. I'm so terribly sor…"

"Shhh…" he stopped me from speaking as I wept. "I'm just so damned happy you're home – and safe. I love you so, Madgie. Shh…"

My face was a wet mess of tears and mucus smearing Pappy's shoulder. We stood for several moments, holding each other. It was hard to breath as his arms were like bands of iron around me, but I couldn't bring myself to draw away.

Suddenly, the front door opened. Startled, I watched over Pappy's shoulder as a man and woman stepped cautiously into the entryway, carrying valises. They blinked as their eyes grew used to the dimness. Both looked travel-worn and tired, glancing around the room. It was the woman who saw us first.

"Oh," she said, staring at us as we were still locked in our embrace.

I noticed for the first time that Pappy smelt unwashed.

This is not the same inn-keeper who thinks forever of what might please a guest.

"Welcome to the Gander's Wing of Trivington," I said, releasing and stepping away from Pappy, though he grasped at my hand. Another chunk of tart crust fell from my bodice to the floor.

"Please forgive us as we are terribly happy after a horrible fright. The guest rooms are tidy," I said, then laughed, motioning toward my front. "Tidier than us at any rate! For a shilling deposit, I can show you to a fine private room, or a bed in the Commons for a penny per guest."

The man looked at me doubtfully, clutching his valise tightly.

"Regardless of how it may appear, we are not daft," I continued, dabbing my face with my sleeve. "You will be quite safe and comfortable should you stay, I assure you."

Pappy had moved away from me and lowered himself slowly back down into the chair, his elbows resting on his knees.

Though the man still looked uneasy, the woman smiled slightly and began to smooth her hair into place, saying, "Please, John. I am so tired of being in that horrible carriage."

Sighing, the man reached for a coin purse at his belt.

"A private room, please," he said, pulling the drawstrings open. "Preferably one with a looking glass should you have it."

"Right this way," I said, heading toward the stairs.

Ah! Such lovely stairs! I thought as my feet ascended them. Down the hall we trekked, and I ran my hand along the wall, my heart bursting. Opening the door, I stepped into the room, the couple right behind me.

Looking Glass Room! I shall be happy to tidy you on the morrow.

The couple glanced around the room, seeming pleased at what they saw. The woman sank onto the bed with a sigh.

"Supper is served at sunset in the dining room."

I must get down to the kitchen to help Babs in preparing that. Glancing down at my hands and clothes, I nearly giggled. *Well, after I wash, I suppose.*

I caught sight of myself in the looking glass. The sun was shining in through the window brightly, a beam of it falling across my face and body. Turning fully toward the mirror, I tucked a lock of hair behind my ear that I might better see the face so like my mother's.

The greyish green eyes looked steadily back at me, just as they were learning to at others. Below them was the mouth that could now sing before throngs of people without clamping shut in fear. And of course, on my left cheek was my birthmark, red and rough as ever, but there was a smile beneath it.

"Yer pretty. Well, at least y'are when yer smilin'..."

Yes, Brom. I am *pretty.*

Holding my head high, I turned back to the guests.

"Please ring the bell at the desk if you have need of anything."

With one final glance at the mirror, I turned to leave, so thankful to be home.

So very happy and thankful.

The End

After Words

A Clarification...

A century or so before the founding of the Friends (Quakers) by George Fox, it was common for English speakers to use the pronouns 'thee' and 'thou'. According to my research, that had changed by the end of the 17th century except for in the northern areas of England. One thing that distinguished the Quakers from non-Quakers in historical Southern England was their constant use of 'thee' and 'thou' to promote egalitarian thinking and treatment amongst all sectors of society.

The King James Bible was translated between 1604 and 1611 and includes plenty of thees and thous. It is believed that these pronouns were used in order to preserve the sense of the original Hebrew and Greek even though they were falling out of use in everyday speech.

Many heartfelt thanks to...

...my crew of beta-readers: Lona, Jeff, Ruthie, George, Rene, Tobias and Delaney. Your suggestions on how to alter this story were invaluable and I appreciate all of you so much!

...my beloved husband for allowing me to completely hog the computer for the last seven months. ❤ Now you can have it...for a while.

...Lona Manning, author of the outstanding books *A Contrary Wind* and *A Marriage of Attachment* (Jane Austen fans, seek these titles out on Amazon!) for reading *A Girl Called Foote*, writing a review of it and then cyber-stalking me into a delightfully symbiotic relationship. Your help with *this* novel was much appreciated.

...Julie Hopkins, cover designer extraordinaire. Your willingness to tweak even minor aspects of the cover to fulfill my wishes was admirable, and the end result is gorgeous. (Need a book cover? Visit: https://www.indiebookcoverdesign.com/)

...Christopher Nick Hansen, the designer of Beyond Wonderland, which is the beauteous title font on this book's cover. Thank you, Chris for creating a font that conveys so much of the human experience with just a few shapes and lines.

...my daughter for formatting the 65,000+ words upon these pages.

...Samuel Pepys, the long-dead yet prolific diarist whose writings give us countless interesting glimpses into how life was lived in England 350 years ago.

...the people at MerriamWebster.com who provided me with hours of entertainment as I researched words to ensure they were even in existence at the time that Madge would utter or think them.

…Deanna Jenson of Badon Hill for posting a tutorial on how to make a pair of leather shoes on her Annales Historiae blog. Though I didn't take the time to fashion my own pair, your guidance enabled me to envision Yates doing so.

Apologies to…

…anyone who has or has had a physical trait similar to those described in these pages who felt dissatisfied at their presentation. One of my main points in writing this story was to portray those who look a bit different in a dignified and appreciable light. If, in your estimation, I failed at this, please know that my intentions were good and I did my best as a faulty human being with limited understanding and resources.

…Quakers everywhere. Sorry that the main representative of your community in this book was rather obnoxious. Every Friend I've ever had the pleasure of meeting was a kind and thoughtful person. I've thought much on Thrin's whole story and perhaps will someday write it out that others can understand her better and possibly extend grace to her even as she shushes birds all the way home.

…true historians who detect inaccuracies within this story. But keep in mind, I am a *creative* writer.

...any reader who is bothered that this story concluded without various characters making second appearances. This was *Madge's* story and I felt that to bring some people back later on would detract from that. Still, I imagine some of you are upset with me that a certain young Huguenot girl (and perhaps others) didn't reappear in the final chapters. Sorry!

Enthusiastic invitations to anyone who enjoyed this book to...

...*please* write an honest review of it on Amazon and/or Goodreads. Few things please me more than to see evidence that someone-somewhere liked the book that I toiled and fretted over for months and months. The review can be as short as *one* sentence! Thank you in advance.

...suggest my novels to book clubs, libraries and book stores. I'm not looking to get rich so much as I am looking to simply get read. Thanks!

...get ahold of my first novel, *A Girl Called Foote*, available on Amazon. The blurb for it is as follows:

Young Jonathan Clyde causes mischief for everyone at Whitehall, the stately home of his privileged ancestors. As he matures, however, he comes to despise the vanity and conceit surrounding him.

Misfortune requires Lydia Smythe, an exceptionally clever farmer's daughter, to seek employment at Whitehall. As a parlor maid, she feels stifled and harried by those over her. Still, she refuses to relinquish her independent mind and spirit.

From the moment Jonathan catches Lydia reading the books she is supposed to be dusting, he is intrigued by this unusual servant. Thus begins a clandestine relationship that is simultaneously amusing, confusing and enlightening. Just as it is evolving into something neither of them expected, an unforeseen truth comes to light, and the two wonder if their unconventional bond will be forever lost.

Set in England in the mid-eighteen hundreds, *A Girl Called Foote* is the coming-of-age story of two similarly impressive people leading very different lives.

An excerpt from *A Girl Called Foote,* also by A.E. Walnofer

Due to a scuttling rat in the floorboards of his bedroom, Jonathan had not slept well the night before. Following breakfast, he wandered into the library for his sketchbook but soon found himself curled up on the settee.

Ah yes, the old napping place, he thought, grabbing a nearby decorative pillow. *Hello. You've cradle my weary head before. In fact, I do believe that's a spot from my drooling mouth from ages ago. Ah, soft as ever.*

What seemed like only moments later, the cramping of his knees and the sound of a door closing awoke him from his light nap.

Who's that? he thought dully.

The newest servant girl came into view.

Ah, the Retriever of Fallen Teeth.

She went directly to the bookshelf ladder, dust rag in hand, and ascended it.

Servants, Jonathan considered, looking at the girl through barely opened eyes. *They appear magically when one tugs the bell pull...or simply to awaken one from a much-needed nap.*

Jonathan thought back on the times he had played tricks on various servants, recalling how sometimes they were amused along with him, and other times seemed angry in a silent, constipated way.

Most of the servants employed at Whitehall were either mere children or, what Jonathan considered, old. Once he had heard his mother say that young men ate far too much and young women were a distraction to the men so neither would be chosen to serve in her home.

Yet, here is a girl about the age of Sophia, newly hired. Perhaps the Lady supposed this particular girl would not tempt the men of the household. Though I'm not sure why, thought Jonathan. *She's reasonably pretty.*

A number of his fellow Heath students had bragged about conquests they'd made of their families' various maids, both attractive and plain. Most of the stories were, Jonathan thought, based on the unimpressive nature of their tellers, highly exaggerated at best and completely fictitious at worst, but a few were plausible.

This girl had dark hair and a figure that was slender without appearing juvenile. Though Jonathan had not seen much of her face, which was presently turned away from him, he recalled it having a nose that was a little short and a chin that was a little broad.

Groggily, Jonathan watched as she put down the dust rag and proceeded to do something very strange.

His eyes flew wide open, though he remained lying still on the settee.

Did she just take a book from her apron pocket and return it to the shelf?

His interest piqued, he watched intently to see what else she might do.

The girl hummed a tune quietly as she resumed dusting shelf after shelf. Suddenly, she stopped, saying, "Oh!"

She lifted another book which Jonathan recognized, flipped through several pages and began to read, perched on the ladder. A few years earlier, he had looked through the same book. Upon opening it, he had had little motivation to comprehend the poems. The inscrutable Scottish dialect had muddled his brain.

Jonathan held his breath, aware even of the sound his eyelashes made against the pillow as he blinked, watching for several moments, delighted and astonished.

A servant girl who reads Robert Burns?

The girl turned a page and quietly giggled.

Is it possible she understands and likes that jumble of words?

Taking something small from her pocket, she put it between the pages and returned the book to its place. Two shelves later, she lifted another book and began to flip through it.

Amused, Jonathan could stay silent no longer.

"Getting the dust from between the pages?"

Her reaction was similar to what Ploughman's had been to the flatus he passed many years earlier in the very same room --a frantic clutching of the ladder and wild turnings of the head.

When she had regained composure, she replied, stiffly, "Sorry, sir. I didn't see you there."

"That's quite clear." He sat up and stretched enormously.

She pushed the book, which miraculously had not dropped from her hand, back into place and resumed dusting, vigorously. Silence prevailed as she finished cleaning the final bookcase.

As she returned the book ladder to its place, Jonathan asked, "Do you really understand the poems of Robert Burns?"

The girl assumed the uncomfortable air that servants often did when Jonathan asked them questions. They would answer him politely, but with a steeliness under the words and facial expression that made him think they just wanted to be done with him.

"I'm able to discern enough to find enjoyment in them," she replied after a brief pause.

Jonathan felt the corners of his mouth twitching.

Did this parlor maid just use the word 'discern'?

"You're the 'new Foote', aren't you?" He studied her and saw he had been correct about her face. None of the features were noteworthy, but none were unfavorable. Her eyes were light, though he couldn't tell if they were blue, gray or green from the distance. He also noticed two moles on the left side of her face.

"So says the Lady," she said, then bit her lip and quickly added, "Sir, would you like me to go until you're finished with this room?"

Slightly taken aback, Jonathan said, "Yes. Yes, I would."

Quickly, Foote gathered her cleaning materials and left.

After the door had shut behind her, Jonathan sat for a moment longer, marveling.

'So says the Lady'? Sounds as if she's been familiarized with the Lady's charms. But what an odd servant--stowing books in her apron and marking pages of poetry! What page was that that made her giggle? he wondered, standing and moving toward the shelf.

Holding the book loosely in his hand, it fell open to where a torn scrap of paper had been placed.

Why, it's the haggis!

He nearly laughed.

That was the only poem in the book that I somewhat enjoyed as it celebrated something so vile.

There in the margin, next to the title "Address to a Haggis" was a little sketch of a platter overwhelmed by a hulking, steaming sheep-gut. Just beyond was a man's overly large grotesque face, split with a wide grin. In his raised hands, he held a knife and a fork as if he was about to greedily devour the entire sausage-like bag.

Ahh, yes, I remember drawing this. I'm still quite pleased with the rendition.

He silently read the first two lines:

Fair fa' your honest, sonsie face

Great chieftain o the puddin'-race!

*Hmmm...*he pondered. *Was it the poem or my drawing that made her laugh?*

He shut the book and returned it to its shelf, a small smile on his lips.

***

Out in the hallway, Lydia bit her lip. *Is he always going to catch me looking through books?*

The thought was interrupted by the sound of quick, punctuated footsteps coming down the hall.

Ugh...Smith, always treading about...

Setting the bucket down roughly, Lydia grabbed a rag and began to dust the frames of the William Walter Clyde portraits, or 'those Clyde Fellows' as she had come to think of them. Her heart was still pounding from her exchange with the young baronet.

Did he see me returning Rob Roy to the shelf?

A shiver of fear ran through her stomach.

What if he did dismiss me?

Don't be ridiculous! He didn't seem bothered in the least. In fact, he seemed... entertained. Is that the right word? Maybe, but whatever it was, it wasn't anger or disgust. This thought settled her a bit as Smith's footsteps grew louder.

Can't he go nap in his room? Isn't that what a bed is for?
I've been looking forward to dusting those books all week!

Lydia hadn't expected Smith, who was always rushing around in every direction, to halt right next to her.

She stopped dusting and looked up. Smith's attention was normally engaged on anything but the person to whom she spoke, so Lydia found it strange to be staring into her lightly lashed blue eyes.

"Foote?"

"Yes?"

"It's Thursday," Smith said in a low voice.

The words hung in the air meaninglessly. Having no idea what her expected response ought to be, Lydia repeated, "Yes?"

Smith's mouth puckered sourly as she pointed at the door nearest them. "It's library-and-study-day, not hallway-day. I'm sure there's plenty to be done in there." She began to reach for the doorknob.

"The baronet desires to be alone." Lydia regretted saying the words instantly, imagining Smith bursting in on the young man and having her own awkward interaction with him.

That would have been fun to watch.

"Oh..." Smith's hand fell to her side and her mouth opened and shut a couple of times.

Ha! You've nothing to say to that, have you? Lydia could feel the smugness of her thoughts squaring and lifting her shoulders as she faced the elder woman.

Seeming to sense it, Smith sniffed and looked Lydia over head to toe.

"Where is your mob-cap, Foote?"

"My mob-cap?" Lydia felt her confidence wane.

Where is that hideous thing?

She felt around and pulled the limp, crumpled hat from a small pocket on her bodice.

"Because you've been caught improperly attired, you will lose your free afternoon this Sunday."

"*What?!*" Lydia gasped, her mouth hanging open.

Smith continued quietly, "It is vital that you represent the family well by wearing the designated uniform."

"Yes," Lydia spat, holding her hands out to indicate the empty hallway, "in front of this *vast array* of witnesses."

"Don't make it *two* Sundays, Foote." Smith's voice was low and fierce. "There's plenty of silver to be polished again and again. Now put that on and get to work."

Her quick, clipped footsteps began again, sounding down the hallway and rounding the corner.

Lydia stood aghast.

How can she...?

I didn't know she'd... Ugh!

She pulled the hat onto her head hard enough to hear a stitch give.

It's just going to fall off without the pins.

She found one pin, digging it out of the same pocket and turned to the frame on the wall habitually as if it were a mirror.

Sir William the Second looked back at her, painted as if he smelled a slightly unpleasant odor.

Instinctively, she sneered back and began to rub the rag over his frame, noticing that the caricature face had been removed. A few fibers of paper were stuck to the paint.

I'll probably be required to clean those off, too, she thought, peevishly.

Just then, the library door opened and Sir Jonathan emerged. Not even glancing in her direction, he walked past, straightening his coat and went down the hall, out of sight.

Flustered and angry, Lydia returned to the library with her supplies. Once inside, she shut the door and looked behind all the furniture and in every corner.

Is the little one tormenting a dormouse under the table? Perhaps the Lady is crouching behind the end table, ready to pounce on anyone whose name displeases her.

Satisfied at the room's emptiness, she walked past the settee where Sir Jonathan had been napping. His sketchbook now occupied the place. It was open, but she stayed far enough away as to not see what was on the page.

Is this an invitation or a trap?

She envisioned Sir Jonathan lurking for a moment at the other side of the door and then bursting in, bellowing, "Unhand that book, underling!"

I won't do it, she decided, turning her back on the book, then gasped.

The man with the haggis! He must have drawn that as well!

She giggled at the remembrance of the rapturous look on the man's face.

Well, even if he is a bit pompous and sly, Sir Jonathan is entertaining. She sighed. *But back to work.*

Lydia tended to her cleaning tasks, though she kept glancing at the settee and the book it held. Once she had finished with the parlor and returned her supplies, except for a single dust rag, to the bucket, she looked toward the door and cautiously approached the book.

He wouldn't have put it here if he didn't intend for me to have a look.

She halted, stunned in delighted surprise.

On the page before her was sketched an elderly man with puckered lips, his mouth an empty black hole. A young woman in a maid's garb stood before him, one hand presenting him with a silver platter, the other hand lifting the large silver lid. Upon the platter was a set of teeth as white and gleaming as the cream-colored paper would allow.

That's me! She chuckled silently, studying the sketched maid. Never before had she seen a drawing of herself, at least not from the hand of a talented artist. She recognized some likenesses, but the focus of the drawing was the elderly man. The look of delight on his saggy face was accentuated by the way his hands were thrown out to the sides. His eyes were lit up with unmistakable joy.

What a lovely antiquated suitor... and those untethered teeth!

A feeling Lydia had not experienced for months warmed her, filling her with a quiet sense of excitement. She ached as the long-absent sentiment of understanding another's amusement washed over her.

Words ran through Lydia's mind arranging and rearranging themselves as she continued to stare and giggle. Realizing she would soon be expected back in the kitchen to serve the noon-time meal, she sighed and walked away from the book to leave the room.

It was hours before she realized she had forgotten to slip another book into her apron pocket.

To read Jonathan and Lydia's story in its entirety, please visit Amazon where you will find both eBooks and paperbacks of *A Girl Called Foote* available for purchase.

Made in the USA
San Bernardino, CA
28 June 2018